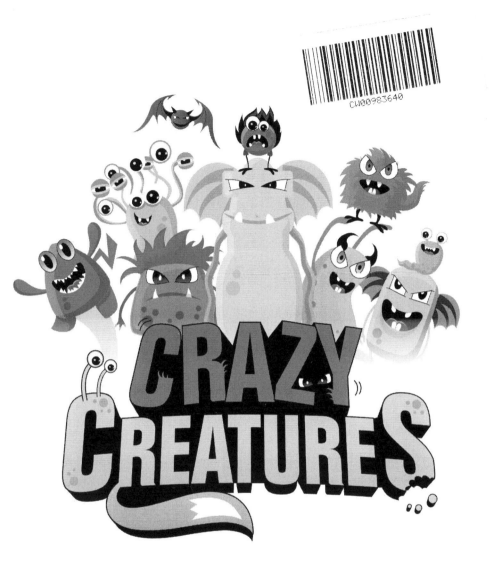

CRAZY CREATURES

UK AUTHORS

Edited By Lynsey Evans

First published in Great Britain in 2024 by:

 Young**Writers**
Est. 1991

Young Writers
Remus House
Coltsfoot Drive
Peterborough
PE2 9BF
Telephone: 01733 890066
Website: www.youngwriters.co.uk

FOREWORD

Welcome Reader!

Are you ready to discover weird and wonderful creatures that you'd never even dreamed of?

For Young Writers' latest competition we asked primary school pupils to create a creature of their own invention, and then write a mini saga about it - a hard task! However, they rose to the challenge magnificently and the result is this fantastic collection full of creepy critters and bizarre beasts!

Here at Young Writers our aim is to encourage creativity in children and to inspire a love of the written word, so it's great to get such an amazing response, with some absolutely fantastic stories.

Not only have these young authors created imaginative and inventive creatures, they've also crafted wonderful tales to showcase their creations. These stories are brimming with inspiration and cover a wide range of themes and emotions - from fun to fear and back again!

I'd like to congratulate all the young authors in this anthology, I hope this inspires them to continue with their creative writing.

CONTENTS

Farsley Springbank Junior School, Farsley

Erin Boyle (9)	50
Emily Porritt (8)	51
Noah Priestley (9)	52
Natalia Abnar (11)	53
Iris Smith (9)	54
Finley Hunt (9)	55
Mathilda Littlewood-Wilcock (11)	56
Evelyn Barrett (10)	57
Elli Hall (9)	58
Evelyn Coop (8)	59
Violet Windle (9)	60
Ava Pallagrass (8)	61
Morgan Chadwick (9)	62
Elsa Scott (9)	63
Isaac Durham (9)	64
Aria Vargerson (9)	65
Alice Lofthouse (9)	66
Ava Lilley (8)	67
Amelia Wilcock (10)	68
Elizabeth Grace Carter (8)	69
Bethany Todd (11)	70
Samuel Wicks (8)	71
Seth Woodside (9)	72
Tilly Davies (10)	73
Alfie Winters (9)	74
Elliot Samuels (8)	75
Emily Housley (7)	76
Zack Habib (9)	77
Prudence McGarry (10)	78
Quorra Downing (9)	79
Luna Moore (7)	80

Freeland CE Primary School, Freeland

Timily Cripps (7)	81

Grouville Primary School, Grouville

Ayla Hawgood (10)	82

Alanis McCarroll (11)	83
Ned Monahan (11)	84
Erin Troy (11)	85
Noah Monahan (11) & Buddy Sharkey (10)	86
Jake Kelly (10)	87
William Austin (11) & Saul Brennan (11)	88
Daisy Campbell	89
Nina Mousdale (11)	90
Lyra McKeown (11)	91
Indie Roberts (10)	92
Maddison de Loynes (10)	93
Mae Jackson (10)	94
Henry Skrivelis (11) & Finley Norbury (11)	95
Noah Camara	96
Andre Camacho (11)	97
Eva De Castro (10) & Amelia Linstead (10)	98
Charlotte Wiltcher Woodman (11)	99
Nina Kordzinska (11)	100
Maiyah-Sophie Misson (11)	101

Hertford Junior School, Hollingdean

Lily M (8)	102
Leah D (10)	103

Ivy House School, Golders Green

Hannah Farrell (9)	104
Alanna Ramchandani (9)	105
Vanessa Edde (10)	106
Arina Nemodruk (10)	107
Lavinia Marsh (9)	108

James Cambell Primary School, Dagenham

Briken Mia (10)	109
Maisha Hussain (11)	110
Hephzibah Adedayo (10)	111
Jannah Hossain (10)	112

Aarya Bancey (11)	113
Holly Wingate (10)	114
Zeenat Adeniran (10)	115
Ellie-Mae Sullivan (10)	116
Yusef Ali (10)	117
Millie Soane (11)	118
Lily Gladman (11)	119
Shakina Boodhoo (11)	120
Bilal Brika (10)	121
Leonel Syla (11)	122
Eve Ellis (11)	123
Michelle Thompson (11)	124
Ramina Gawau (10)	125
Mia Barclay (11)	126
Olivia Umeh (9)	127
Kapilan Ketheeswaran (11)	128
Baalis Odofin (10)	129
Ryan Cole (10)	130
Evie-Mae Sutton (10)	131
Shah-Aayan Ahmed (10)	132
Charlie Tyler (10)	133
Favour O-Oluwasemilore (11)	134
Henry Rayner (11)	135
Isla Mursell (11)	136
Fraser McCarthy (11)	137
Poppy Rawlinson (10)	138
Castiel Trench	139
Freya Ellis (10)	140
Ahmed Suleyman (10)	141
Tyler Sims (11)	142
John Alogba (11)	143
Akachuwku Onuorah (10)	144

Rochester Riverside CE Primary School, Rochester

David Onyenwenu (8)	145
Sofia Georgieva (7)	146
Matthew Sutch (7)	147
Reese Agoro (8)	148
Noemi Astorri (8)	149
Lorcàn Steele (7)	150
Ismé Nkansah (8)	151
Ruby Foster (7)	152

St Peter's Primary School, Newry

Bronwyn McCabe (10)	153
Lexi Kennedy (9)	154
Elisha Duffy (10)	155
Noel Anderson (10)	156
Ava Powell (9)	157
Gabrielle Lowe (10)	158
Evie Canavan (9)	159
Conor Marron (9)	160
Alice Johnston (10)	161
Tommy McGlade (9)	162
Katie McGivern (10)	163
Sonia Olszowy (10)	164
Adaeze Obidike (9)	165
Chloe Carragher (10)	166
Kieran Fitzpatrick (10)	167
Eve Connolly (10)	168
Michael Magill (10)	169

St Teresa's Primary School, St Helens

Addison Balmer (10)	170
William Hobin (10)	171
Aya (9)	172
Lucas Roscoe (10)	173
Rejoice Ose-Ose Ebhodaghe (10)	174
Joseph Leigh (10)	175

Stifford Clays Primary School, Stifford Clays

Blessing Folarin (10)	176
Abigail Anyia (10)	177
Gracie Cook (9)	178
Amber Waterman (10)	179
Holly Seabrook (10)	180
Rosie Austen (10)	181
Poppy Atkin (10)	182
Annie Smith (10)	183

Voyage Learning Campus, Worle

Tara-Leigh Morris (6)	184
JJ Murray (7)	185
Lucifer McMillan (7)	186
Lexi-Louise Chivers (7)	187
Luke Baker (10)	188

THE STORIES

I Want To Play For Liverpool

One day Dandy, an alien from Liverpool Land, went to Anfield and asked Jürgen Klopp if he could play for Liverpool. "No," said Jürgen Klopp, "you can't play football."
"Can I go in goal then?"
"No, your arms are too wobbly." So Dandy went back to Liverpool Land.
The next day Dandy went to Anfield and found Luis Díaz playing football, so he joined in. Dandy dribbled past Luis Díaz and scored lots of goals against him. Then Jürgen Klopp came in and saw Dandy playing. He was amazed, so he let Dandy play for Liverpool.

Jess Spragg (8)
Betley CE Primary School, Betley

1

Winter Love

Once upon a time there was a little creature, her name was Violet and one day Violet left the palace for one night, then went back to Winter Wonderland where she lived. Anyway, she went back to her house. The Queen, her mum, didn't recognise her. She said, blushing, "Who are you?" Then Violet was also blushing. Then she said, "I am your daughter, Violet." She burst out crying. Her mum said, "Stop crying over nothing, you aren't even Violet." But then all of a sudden the mum noticed who Violet was. The mum felt very sorry that she screamed at her.

Sylvie Michael (7)
Betley CE Primary School, Betley

Untitled

Once upon a monster, there was a little monster called Sunny. One day, her mam told her, "Sunny, you are going to Monster High."
"Yeaahh!" She'd always wanted to go to Monster High.
"You will go on the twenty-first of May this year. Right now, it is the thirtieth of April."
"Okay Mum, I'll go and start packing."
Over the next few weeks, she was saying goodbye. Finally, the day had come. As she set off, a girl came up to her. She started saying nasty words to her. Sunny stood up for herself. Everyone was brave.

Harriet Thompson (7)
Betley CE Primary School, Betley

3

The Cup

Our story starts in Bobblybingbo's house. Bobblybingbo was eating ice cream and playing Fortnite. He remembered it was the Manchester Derby in the cup!

"Oh no!" he said. "I must sneak in."

So he hopped on his motorbike, sped past all the traffic and got pulled over by the police.

The police said, "Who are you?"

He said, "I'm Bobblybingbo with five eyeballs, arms of a yeti, legs of a tarantula and teeth of a vampire."

After, he just sped off. The game ended 7-2. He celebrated. He was a Man City fan.

Bobby Hoskins (8)
Betley CE Primary School, Betley

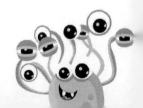

The Lindor Chocolate Plot!

Lindy was a little monster. She grew up with the new Volcano King on Planet Gold-way. They soon became enemies.

One day, Lindy was thinking about this. She decided to pay him a visit and use her Lindor Chocolate Powers to pelt them at him, and that's exactly what she did.

She arrived at the volcanoes and saw him. She went up to him and said, "You have terrorised monsters long enough. Time for you to pay the price!"

"Ha! I'll rule the world!" he said.

She shot her Lindors and, *poof!* He was gone for good. Job done!

Maya Srejic (9)
Betley CE Primary School, Betley

Fighting Robots

Basher had just left school and was walking home with his friends when he saw a group of robots. Robots were their worst enemies. Suddenly, one of the robots shouted, "Surrender, you're surrounded!"

Then Basher charged at one of the robots and sent him flying into a building. Then all of his friends copied him. Soon, all the robots were broken, but the broken robots joined together and made one big robot! Basher charged at it, but it didn't even dent. Then all his friends charged at the robot and broke it. Then all his friends ran home together.

Thomas Brindle (9)
Betley CE Primary School, Betley

Creature Craziness

Once, an alien from Hoppy Land was about to swing to victory on Gladiators when Mark Clattenberg blew his whistle to stop. Everyone was very confused. Mark explained that Timmy Topps was biting Summple's leg so he would restart the eliminator and Summple would get a thirty-minute head start.

Of course, Summple won by twenty-nine minutes and fifty-nine seconds. He had won the finals of Gladiators. Timmy Topps could not take this. How was Summple so fast? Summple had known Timmy Topps since primary school. He knew Timmy Topps was about to *attack!*

Henry Griffiths (9)
Betley CE Primary School, Betley

7

Crazy The Liverpool Fan

Once upon a time, there was a little monster called Crazy, and he loved Liverpool. One day he was watching a Liverpool match, and just as they were about to score, he got a call. It was from Liverpool, and they said, "You are the star customer. You can go to the VIP seats."

He said, "Okay."

Then he cut off. He was so excited that he sprinted to the seats. They were so comfortable; he loved it because they won, and when he got home, he watched the highlights, and his favourite player scored all the goals, five-nil.

Henry Jones (8)
Betley CE Primary School, Betley

The Trip To London

Lola was an adorable, friendly monster who loved to explore. One day, Lola climbed into her space rocket. Her rocket was as shiny as the sun blazing on a piece of sparkly metal. Lola was terrible at driving - really, really bad. Eventually, she arrived in London. Lola went on a walk. She saw the London Eye so she bravely decided to go on it. Did I mention Lola hated heights? Then she went to Big Ben. She loved the noise. Next, she found a red London bus parked next to her space rocket. "Back to Pluto, I go!" she exclaimed.

Pippa Sheldon (7)
Betley CE Primary School, Betley

Rainbow Was Born

I'm Handstand Rainbow. When I was born, my dad was in a war and died against Planet Gold. You could hear the guns being shot. We went out of the hospital; it was smoky and smelled like gunpowder. It was a sad time. Planet Gold took over the whole town. We were frightened to move into a little mushroom home to live in. When I was five years old, Mum got me a pet called Buttercup. Mum died when I was six years old. Planet Gold struck again! I punched it, and they were all gone. Planet Gold was never seen again. It was me and Buttercup.

Evy Kirkham (9)
Betley CE Primary School, Betley

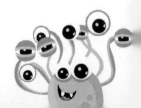

Portvale's Revenge

One day, there was a guy called Stevey Stoke. He had a great idea to use his time machine, so off he went, but when he was travelling, suddenly, *bang!* He went into the Shatterverse world. First, he went into New Yoke City, but his enemies were there, the Portvale Guys; they were taking over the world. He was not going to let that happen. He went for the kill. After a long fight, he won and noticed they had a paradox prism. He took it and went back home, winning and celebrating, juggling his bananas, but they might come back...

Will Beeston (8)
Betley CE Primary School, Betley

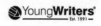
Wockings Is A Villa Fan

Wockings is a Villa fan. He loves, I mean *loves*, Aston Villa. All he wears are Aston Villa clothes. He was born next to Villa Park. He is the best footballer in the world because he knows the best tricks and skills.

He wants to play for Aston Villa, but he can't because footballers can only be human, not creatures. He does not want to play against Ederson because he is the best goalie, but Wockings is the best forward, so he goes.

They say no, but Wockings does not give up. He dresses up as a human.

Freddy Crawford (8)
Betley CE Primary School, Betley

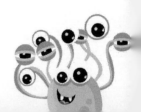

Planet Peril

Once, there was an alien called Flafals and he could inflate himself. One day on Planet Flafels, food was missing and the Raters could only do it. Flafals sneaked into Rater Town, he turned a corner and Raters came charging but Flafals inflated himself, bouncing them away. In front of him was a maze, he wandered through and found a map and located the food. So Flafals bounced back the food for all the aliens. When he got back home he was remembered as the hero of Planet Flafals and was very proud of himself.

Nikolas Srejic (9)
Betley CE Primary School, Betley

13

Planto And The Annoying Flies

Once, in a place as old as time, a strange peculiar creature hatched from Venus. After a few years, the creature grew up and got named, and his name was Planto. Also, he was a spider squid. He always wanted to plant a seedling, he was obsessed with planting. At this point, I should probably mention that Planto hates flies, and he wanted to plant but a fly would eat the plant. So he decided to buy a flycatcher. So he did, but he didn't know where so he just put it next to the rainbow daffodils he grew.

Edith Bettley (7)
Betley CE Primary School, Betley

Coral War

One early, warm summer morning, Dave the diver was up and noticed he was late for work! Then he remembered he worked on his own.

Suddenly, he heard a little knock on his door. It was Bloop but, surprisingly, there was just a letter. He opened it and it said, 'I'm sorry I've been so mean. I want to work with you now.'

He thought to himself, *finally! Someone to work with.*

The next morning, they worked together and they loved it, so they agreed to do it from then on.

Harry Spence (8)
Betley CE Primary School, Betley

Rosey And The Story

Rosey was asleep. Suddenly, she heard something weird and the floor turned blue and black. Then she fell out of her bed. She turned part bear and part sloth and part unicorn. "What's happening to me? Maybe it's a dream? I'm going to make the most of it while I'm here!"

She heard some weird noises then she saw a little twinkle and she followed it to her house. She got back to her house.

The alarm clock went off and she woke up. It must have been a dream!

Lulu Rimmer (7)

Betley CE Primary School, Betley

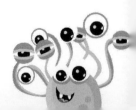

Angel And Her Friend

Angel is a little bit naughty and she doesn't have any friends. When she tries to laugh, people think she is scaring the people around her, so she gets in her car and goes home.

She goes to the park to find a friend. There is a sad monster on the swing and Angel makes friends with her. They plan to be friends forever.

One day, she meets her again in the same place. At first, they do not recognise each other but, after a few looks, Angel knows it is her friend.

Marloe Dyer (8)
Betley CE Primary School, Betley

The Chase Of The Creatures

One day, Seal floated out of his bed and started his routine. He unplugged himself and then he put his laser hat on so he could shoot intruders if any came. Seal went to work in the futuristic city as a guard so no one could break in, but Stas came and Seal and Stas went on a chase in the city. The jets underneath them propelled them into the air. Seal had a laser hat on the top of his head! He missed with ten of his lasers but then he got Stas and it was all over.

Tom Bethell (9)

Betley CE Primary School, Betley

Dee's Dream Diary

Saturday: Hi, my name's Dee. It's my first day at school, but not just any school - a hammer-throwing school. You see, being a hammer champion is my dream and I've been training hard. Oh! The games are starting. Bye.
Sunday: I won! I won! Hooray!
Monday: School's been hard lately. Douglas's gang were getting angry. They went crazy and attacked everyone. Suddenly, I had an idea. I threw my hammer and, *bash!* I saved the day!

Finn Fletcher (9)
Betley CE Primary School, Betley

Untitled

My monster is called Sophia. She is kind, she is from Betley. She wants to go to Betley School but she can't because she is not a human. She goes to a magic place to be a human. The lady is called Miss Lucy. She says, "Of course I can make you into a human. Do you want to be a human forever?" Sophia says yes. She goes to the school and she makes friends called Ella and Lulu and Grace and Eliza. Ella says hi to Sophia. Sophia says hi to Ella.

Gracie Dowley (8)
Betley CE Primary School, Betley

Rich People

One day the monster world changed. Jess, the happy monster that danced and snowboarded, she loved everyone she saw. But one day she moved to Manchester and became a star. So she had children with her husband and they became the royal monster family. They had five maids, seven bakers and nine security.

But one day her husband died, until she had the power to bring him back to life, so no one would ever die. They were happy and close together.

Hattie Smith (7)
Betley CE Primary School, Betley

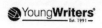

Noobanoobo Gets A Job

Noobanoobo wanted a job. He got an interview, but he didn't know English, so he learnt it. It took two days, seven hours, five minutes and twenty-seven seconds to learn all of it.

He went back and got the job. The role was a chef, but he didn't like it, so he quit and got another job and he loved it. He was an engineer.

He got married and had a baby. Two years later, the baby was starting to walk and talk.

Theo Daly (8)
Betley CE Primary School, Betley

Bobby's And Tom's Adventure

One day, in a big lake there was a boy called Tom. He lived with his two brothers and one sister. Both of Tom's brothers went in a cave and got eaten by a dragon.

The next day Tom said, "Where are my brothers?" Then he saw his friend called Bobby. They got an arrow and shot the dragon in the mouth. Then they shot for ten minutes and made a bigger hole for Tom's brothers to climb out.

Jack Forrest (9)
Betley CE Primary School, Betley

Sweet Shop Silly

Silly is a kind, royal monster and she wants to work at a sweet shop in Trentham Shopping Centre. So the next day she goes to apply for the job. She gets the job. The next day Silly gets her bow tie on and walks to work. She only lives next to Trentham.

When she goes to work she eats all the sweets. She is sick everywhere. After that the manager comes in and says, "Silly, you're fired!"

Tessa Luckock (8)
Betley CE Primary School, Betley

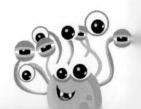

The Adventures Of Blubal And Bon

One day there were two kids. They were called Blubal and Bon. But they had enemies. They were called Fire Dragon and Darth Vader. They killed a hundred people. "We need to kill them, but how? We need to go to the man cave, okay?"
They got a shovel and tunnelled down and got stuck in an amethyst geode. Darth Vader tried to stab Blubal but Bon jumped in and stabbed him.

Thomas Lawton (8)
Betley CE Primary School, Betley

Untitled

Once upon a time, there was a monster called Billy. He was funny and happy. He looked like a blue, bouncy ball.
One day, he went into the woods to collect firewood. He set fire to a tree, got prosecuted, lost his job and went to jail.

Cody Hughes (8)
Betley CE Primary School, Betley

Sam

Sam scares everything and he eats all of his friends. He grows big. He grows bigger and bigger and turns into a fire monster. He can scare anything. The monster screamed because he liked screaming.

Ayesha Tufail (8)
Betley CE Primary School, Betley

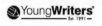

Donker's Life

Donker is made in a lab by a scientist. Then Donker leaves the lab! Then he meets adults and they get scared, then Donkers kills bad monsters and wins!

William Sargent (7)
Betley CE Primary School, Betley

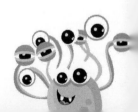

Monster Madness

On Planet Monstrous lived Moonlight, known for shooting lasers out of his eyes. His biggest foe was Bigfoot, known for terrifying children with his invisibility powers.

One day, sitting on Planet Putrid, Bigfoot was planning on terrifying all the children on Planet Monstrous, so they'd pass out and he would own the whole planet. However, Moonlight couldn't let that happen. The day Bigfoot arrived on Planet Monstrous, Moonlight met him face-to-face. The battle had begun. Moonlight started to shoot lasers at him, while Bigfoot jump scared Moonlight. Finally, Moonlight managed to pass him out, and he won.

Aimen Zaidi (10)
Broadford Primary School, Harold Hill

29

A Creature Called Clever Clyde

Once there was a little girl called Luna, she was just admiring how beautiful the sky was, when one day, she saw something unusual. It was swiftly and slowly coming down. Once it arrived she carefully approached it. It was a small spaceship. The doors opened and a small, cute, fluffy creature walked out. The creature was blue, small and shaped like a ball but with two arms and legs. They walked to each other and it turned out to be just a harmless monster called Clever Clyde. Now, every day Luna waits for Clever Clyde to arrive and play together.

Netany Wang (10)
Broadford Primary School, Harold Hill

The Angel And The Devil

Once, there was an angel called Lilly. She was kind and pretty looking. She once went on a walk to the park and saw a devil who was doing naughty things. Lilly went up to the devil, and Lilly said, "What is your name?"
The devil said, "My name is Penny."
Lilly said, "Why did you hurt these innocent people?"
Penny said, "Because I am a devil. I am naughty, and you are a stupid little angel called Lilly, so I will hurt you."
So Penny started to shoot fire at Lilly.
Lilly said, "Can we be friends?"
The devil said, "Yes."

Annabelle Phillips (9)
Brookdale Primary School, Wirral

Stretch Mouth

Meet Stretch Mouth. He's small but mighty. How mighty? He can swallow things as big as a van. I met him the day my mum called the plumber to fix the sink. The plumber went back to her van for her tools, only to find Stretch Mouth sitting in the road where her van should have been. How do we know Stretch Mouth ate the colossal van? you might ask. He burped loudly and we smelled petrol. And don't try to sneak up on him. He showed me his hidden eyes behind his ears. He can see behind himself. How cool is that?

Alexander Howarth (8)
Brookdale Primary School, Wirral

Sophie And Friends

Sophie welcomes a dragon but they topple over the lion and the lion is angry about Sophie and the dragon toppling over him. But Sophie makes a solution. She plays a superhero game but the dragon misses his home and mum in Candy Land. They have an Easter tea. They have a sleepover. Sophie's mum and dad are friends with the lion's parents and the dragon's mum and dad.
In Sophie's diary she says that she has the best friends. She asks to have a picnic and they say yes, of course.

Olivia Gibbons (9)
Brookdale Primary School, Wirral

Billy-Bob The Tickler

There he lies, waiting to strike. Billy-Bob sees your feet dangling down. He tickles and watches you squeal with laughter and squirm around like a monkey.

He sprints away to find his next victim. He spies Caleb standing, unsuspecting. Billy-Bob sets to work, but there is no squeal, just a little chuckle, and no squirming.

Billy-Bob sighs and trudges under a huge, fancy chair with a red velvet cover in the kitchen.

"Well, tickling isn't for everyone, but I can still do it for the people who enjoy it!"

He walks over to a little girl who squeals as he tickles her minuscule feet...

Lottie Crann (9)
Castlefields Primary School, Bridgnorth

The Fart Tug-Of-War

Planet Pong needs Planet Earth's farts. Algom, a local hero, saves the planet from enormous gas waves by harnessing their energy for use on Pong. One day there was a shortage of farts. Algom first thought that Planet Earth had stopped farting. He realised that his enemy, Algobia, was stealing the farts. Algom went into battle with Algobia because he had put all the farts in his spaceship and was about to escape. Algom set the farts alight by using his flammable breath, causing an enormous explosion and shooting Algobia into deep space, restoring peace and energy to Pong.

Jonny Brown (10)
Castlefields Primary School, Bridgnorth

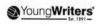

Ogg The Cereal Killer's Final Day

Ogg the Cereal Killer (not from a movie) spent his time pushing other cornflakes into the bowl.
One day, there were no other cornflakes left in the box apart from Ogg. Happy that he had survived, he was soon recycled into another cereal box.
Ogg was soon poured into a breakfast bowl, and as he lay there with other cornflakes, his archnemesis (milk) was poured, covering Ogg and the other cornflakes. Ogg fought, kicking and screaming for his life, but soon a spoon appeared. Ogg spent his final moments on the spoon, ready to be devoured by the human.

Hugo Andrews Madden (10)
Castlefields Primary School, Bridgnorth

Hero From Futurama Saves Earth

Predicto was sent to Earth from his planet, Futurama, to protect the population. He could see a huge earthquake was going to cause devastation for lots of countries, so he knew he had to save Earth.

Predicto's superpower was that he could see into the future. He knew he had to act fast, so he got help from the police, army and emergency services. They got everyone to safety by transporting them to England by boat and plane just in time.

Predicto became an overnight hero and was invited to make his permanent home on Earth.

Alice Allan-Smith (9)

Castlefields Primary School, Bridgnorth

Bread Roll Baddy Strikes

Bread Roll Baddy is a roll born in a bakery in England whose duty is to cause trouble. Bread Roll Baddy's only enemy is Cheese Grain Goody. He really loves to switch ordinary bread rolls and croissants with smelly, out-of-date ones. Quickly, Cheese Grain Goody replaces them with new ones. He absolutely hates all the cheeses. Once Bread Roll Baddy is done, he moves into bakeries so he'll be bought, then he can repeat the process so he can rule the world and maybe even the whole cool, pretty solar system, but where will he strike next?

Jack Wootton (9)
Castlefields Primary School, Bridgnorth

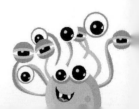

Gobbler's Snack Adventure

Gobbler was hungry, he had been forgotten at the back of the snack cupboard and all the snacks had gone. Cereal was his favourite of all the snacky snacks. He used to wait until breakfast was over before sneaking into the box and eating until he was full as a balloon. Now that the snacks were gone Gobbler had to think of ways to get his sugary snacks snacks. He decided to use his shape-shifting mischievousness to his advantage. He turned into a spoon, found his way into the cutlery drawer and awaited his snacky adventure.

Harvey Broster (10)
Castlefields Primary School, Bridgnorth

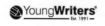

Nitro The Nail Biter's Big Mission

Nitro the nail biter is sent on a wicked mission by his boss. He is told to break into a school and bite the children's fingernails to put in his boss' collection, so that is what Nitro does. He travels carefully to a school, but Nitro's trick is he can turn invisible for ten minutes! So he turns invisible and strolls to a classroom, he sets his eyes on one victim. He scurries to the desk, climbs up the table leg and with the blink of an eye he has his fingernails! He runs out. The mission is completed!

Maddie Kendrick (10)

Castlefields Primary School, Bridgnorth

Monster Scare

One night a little girl called Lilly woke up in fright, she was hearing noises under her old, creepy bed. She quickly shot up to the sky. She was startled because there were five creepy eyes looking at her! She was petrified, she screamed as loud as a lion's roar, but nobody came to her, she had only one chance to climb out of the window, so she did. As she jumped out of the window she slipped, she tried to hold on. Finally she got herself up and went to her mum's room, but the monster was furious!

Darcey Compson-Perks (9)
Castlefields Primary School, Bridgnorth

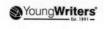

The Darkness Takeover

One dreadful evening, you come home from a long day of work. Then, as you look through the window, you see a figure covered in darkness. When you enter, a big cloud of darkness forms and you are flung into the wall. As you are getting up, it teleports to you and a random spike jabs your hand. Then, after waiting for something crazy to happen, *boom!* A tank made of pure gold bursts through the wall and fires at the creature. Your vision turns black and it disappears. Then you see it.

Jack Green (9)
Castlefields Primary School, Bridgnorth

Bulls Eye's Revenge

Bulls Eye was a very famous warrior. He never lost a war. Sometimes he got shot, but he still lived. One person said he couldn't be real, but he gave them proof he wasn't by surviving a headshot snipe with no protection on his head during a war. When Bulls Eye said one of his war friends had sacrificed his own life to save Bulls Eye by being shot, people were one hundred per cent sure he wasn't a real person. They were shocked. He could have gone to prison.

Finlay Williams (10)
Castlefields Primary School, Bridgnorth

Spidops' Big Move

Once upon a time, Spidops wanted to move from Wales when he turned 18. This was because Wales' weather was so bad that he almost flew away. It meant Spidops had to move for the first time. He lived away from the humans as they were scared of him. But after a few months, he tried again. Some humans saw him. But instead of chasing him, they played tag with him. Spidops won the game of tag, then they played football. It was first to ten. Again, Spidops won!

Alfie Anderson (9)
Castlefields Primary School, Bridgnorth

The Revealing Of The Magical Enchantment

In the heart of a forgotten forest, where shadows danced with whispers of ancient trees, a solitary flame flickered. Its golden glow painted the clearing with an ethereal hue as it caressed the pages of an old leather-bound book. Eager eyes, filled with wonder and longing, traced the words woven in the parchment. With each syllable whispered into the night, the forest stirred, unveiling secrets hidden for aeons. The flame grew brighter, casting away the darkness that cloaked the forgotten tales. In that moment, the world held its breath, as if time paused itself to listen to the story unfolding.

Aisha Adesina (10)
Ealdham Primary School, Eltham

Halloween Night

On one rainy Halloween night, Azula knocked on a door.

"Trick or treat?" she said.

She went to the next house and there she saw a man in a lab costume. He said, "Little girl, follow me and I'll give you lots of sweets!"

Azula nodded joyfully and quickly followed him. He told her to go inside the tube and wait. Then he swiftly pulled the lever...

Clang! Cling!

Azula slowly walked out of the glass tube. She had the horns of a devil, the fangs of a vampire and the wings of a dragon.

He had truly created a child's nightmare.

Jesi Lam (10)
Ealdham Primary School, Eltham

The Story Of Arlong The Galaxy Destroyer

In the vast expanse of the universe, there existed a monstrous being known as Arlong. Arlong was a creature of immense power and destructive capabilities, feared by all who crossed his path. He roamed the galaxies, leaving a trail of devastation in his wake. Arlong's origins were shrouded in mystery, with some claiming he was a creation of dark magic while others believed him to be a force of nature unleashed upon the cosmos. Whatever the truth may have been, one thing was certain: Arlong was a being of pure malice and cruelty intent on bringing chaos wherever he went.

John-Iolo Doe (11)
Ealdham Primary School, Eltham

Untitled

On a lovely Sunday morning, the scary dragon, Stray, went flying to the beautiful castle where Princess Venessa lived. He was so excited to see her but the guard thought he was dangerous and shouted at him to leave. This made Stray angry and unfortunately, he set the palace on fire. Everyone screamed and ran out for safety. Venessa sat on a rock and cried, she was devastated. Stray realised how awful his actions were and immediately went to Venessa to apologise. She forgave him and years later the castle was rebuilt and they lived happily ever after.

Annabelle Harvey (11)
Ealdham Primary School, Eltham

Rainbow Eyes

"Venus are you ready?" said Zelimia.

"Yes Mum," replied Venus.

He knew he was lucky, yet it was only his rainbow eyes that made him invincible. He saw the Kumquat River. He would get the river back.

Two years later...

"I can't believe it's battle day," cried Venus as they got ready. Later, they stepped onto the fresh turf, threatening any dufflepuds near them. Catching sight of the opponent, Venus's power poured out of his eyes. The enemy stumbled and his companions attacked! Venus knew they would win. The field turned red. A cry for victory echoed. The Zeggs had won.

Olivia Katsibas (9)
Eleanor Palmer Primary School, Camden

The Battle Of Heart

The alarm sounded.

"Captain, there's a ship in range!" exclaimed Spark as Captain Galaxy ran up from the lower deck.

"Oh no, it's Sir Rocket. Everybody to your stations. Load the canons."

"Three, two, one..."

Boom!

The sound of the ship exploding was deafening. Then, silence. The crew glanced over to the wreckage and saw a flash of red.

"Oh no, Sir Rocket's still alive!" gasped Captain Galaxy. She created a portal to follow him and hopped in. In no time, she arrived face-to-face with him. "Be gone from this world!"

Boom!

Sir Rocket vanished into thin air forever.

Erin Boyle (9)

Farsley Springbank Junior School, Farsley

The Dance-Off

Blob lived on Planet Boogie, loved to dance, had spots over his tummy, wobbly eyes and crazy hair. Blob's enemy was Captain Banana (CB). They were friends until last year when CB beat Blob for the planet's Best Dancer Award. Blob was heartbroken. He demanded a dance-off. "What? I won that fair and square!" said CB. He eventually agreed, and they jived, spun and hip-hopped. When it was nearly over, Blob morphed into the biggest disco ball ever!

"Wow!" everyone cheered.

"And the winner is... Blob!" In celebration, Blob unexpectedly catapulted CB into outer space and lived happily ever after.

Emily Porritt (8)

Farsley Springbank Junior School, Farsley

Kindness

Zolazoz had just been blasted off his own planet. Scanning the scene around him, he saw a hungry alien. Then he did something he never realised he was capable of. He created a tornado to get rid of the beast! That's right, Zolazoz's skin glowed in a unique way compared to all the other luminescent wonders, then lit up the sky. A vegetarian Spakle (a type of alien) threatened to eat him. The following day, Zolazoz, the curious creature, asked, "Are you okay?"

"No!" he responded. The Spakle explained its emotions, and Zolazoz understood from then, and they became best friends.

Noah Priestley (9)

Farsley Springbank Junior School, Farsley

Monster

A little girl called Stacy was being called names at school, but she never had the confidence to tell a trusted adult. But then she went home, and a mean monster was calling her names. That made Stacy cry herself to sleep. In the morning, the blue monster was joining in with the kids who were calling her names. Stacy had enough.
"Stop, you're hurting my feelings!"
The monster turned pink and walked away. When Stacy came back to school, the monster protected Stacy from the kids. Stacy realised the power of saying no is important to protect herself and staying safe.

Natalia Abnar (11)
Farsley Springbank Junior School, Farsley

Phoenix Feathers

I sat down to watch the game. Contestant one, Icy and Liv, flew through the air as one of the opponents, Skandor and Cassie started swirling around them.

Out of thin air, Smokey and James spat smoke at Icy. She hit the ground and her wing started shrivelling. Everyone watched in horror! Most phoenixes started disappearing when hurt. Icy was out of the game.

"No!"

Skandor the fire phoenix started shooting flames at Smokey. It was over. Skandor and Cassie won. it was a dream! They had been training for years. Never give up, no matter what people say to you.

Iris Smith (9)

Farsley Springbank Junior School, Farsley

Hades And His Evil Plan

On top of Mount Everest lived a naughty, horned creature called Hades and his pet griffin, Lupus, who could shape-shift. At the bottom of the mountain there was a noisy village and every year they celebrated Chinese New Year. They had bright lights, fireworks and - worst of all - irritating music that you could hear from the mountaintop.

This year, Hades had an evil plan. Lupus would shape-shift into a human, set up a stall and sell cakes with sleeping powder in them so that the village people couldn't celebrate New Year for a century.

Will Hades and Lupus succeed?

Finley Hunt (9)
Farsley Springbank Junior School, Farsley

The Mighty Fire Of Flame!

Once upon a time, there lived a girl named Lisa. She lived with her family. One day, Lisa was taking her dog on a walk when she came across something. She didn't know what his 'thing' was so she asked her mum and her mum said, "It's a Fire of Flame. It's *very dangerous!*"
The next day, Lisa saw the Fire of Flame when she was walking. She ran away while screaming. Then, one person who lived in the village got a bucket of water and she threw the bucket on him.
"We're saved!" Lisa shouted.
The monster was never seen again.

Mathilda Littlewood-Wilcock (11)
Farsley Springbank Junior School, Farsley

Worry Of Google World

Google Bug lives in Google World, thwarting the worries of the world. One day, Google Bug goes to the worry web just to find the nefarious Moaner Man.

"Mu ha ha! I will destroy all hope!" he cackles.

"No!" says Google Bug.

"Too late!" he shouts and with a flick of the switch, the worry web's wifi is turned off!

"Oh no!" says the worry spider, head of the worry web.

Suddenly, Google Bug shoots a laser of reassurance destroying the Moaner Man!

"Hip hip hooray!" says the spider. And soon everyone in Google World is happy.

Evelyn Barrett (10)
Farsley Springbank Junior School, Farsley

Wadealone

All you could hear were footsteps. Wadealone was using his power of invisibility to avoid his enemies. He attended the 'All Creatures School' where they often bullied him for being a too-intelligent, gentle creature with not long enough horns and for being too short and fluffy.

This day in particular, Wadealone had had enough and after school, he did something unbelievable. He was always told not to go to the 'other side' but he did. He met a human who told him a magic word to make people like him. It worked and now he is Wade and not Wadealone.

Elli Hall (9)
Farsley Springbank Junior School, Farsley

There Is A Creature In My Bag

There was once an anxious girl called Lilly who went on a trip to Roller Coaster Land. Lilly was scared queuing for one of the rides, she noticed some blue eyes looking at her from her bag. She quickly opened it to see what was inside. To her surprise out popped a little blue creature with four arms, a skinny neck and big claws.

"Who are you?" Lilly asked.

He said, "I'm Inky from Planet Pen. My job is to help children who are nervous about roller coasters, like you."

Inky helped Lilly and they became best friends for the day.

Evelyn Coop (8)
Farsley Springbank Junior School, Farsley

Rosie And The Gentle Giant

Once there was a girl called Rosie who loved travelling. She sailed out to sea and met a monster. The monster's name was Gentle Giant and he could juggle stars.

After a day, they became friends but Rosie was lost. She needed to get home but Gentle Giant helped with that.

After a long journey, it was time to say goodbye.

With a tear rolling down Rosie's cheek, she said, "Goodbye!" and Gentle Giant went sailing away in his boat.

Two years later, Rosie got a letter and inside there was a star from Gentle Giant. She was so happy.

Violet Windle (9)

Farsley Springbank Junior School, Farsley

Space Adventure!

Hi, my name is Ivy, nice to meet you! I'm nine years old and love space. I've got a whole room about it. Oh, and I forgot to tell you that there's something in space that you don't want to see or touch at all, her name is Dark Blood Drop. There have been many warnings about her.

The quest started as I climbed onto the spaceship. 5, 4, 3, 2, 1... blast-off! Ready to defeat the evil creature, wearing my X-ray goggles and gripping my spear. I landed and saw Dark Blood Drop. I raised my spear and *slash!* She was gone forever.

Ava Pallagrass (8)
Farsley Springbank Junior School, Farsley

The Unusual Story Of Death And The Tortoise

A young boy who existed in the atmosphere met a girl. The boy was called Death. An unusual name, but not as unusual as the name Life. There lived a tortoise that was responsible for the fabric of space and time, but thirty years later, Death killed it on his way to the secret door to heaven. Then he heard a rumble. Next, there was a huge crack, like Rice Krispies in the morning. Finally, the world started to crumble, but the tortoise kept holding; his eyes glowed white, and he started levitating while somehow pushing Earth back. The world was saved.

Morgan Chadwick (9)
Farsley Springbank Junior School, Farsley

Space

On Earth, there was a girl called Elsa. She loved space and she loved planets, she loved aliens and she loved everything about space. She even had a book on everything about space.

One day, she was watching TV when there was a sudden warning.

"Dear fellow humans," someone said in a disgusted voice. "We are coming to your planet called Earth."

Even though Elsa loved space, she was scared. Suddenly, a loud noise came from the sky. They were going to destroy the land, so she found a laser and destroyed the aliens.

Elsa Scott (9)
Farsley Springbank Junior School, Farsley

Food And The Many Pikmins

When you're having your food, Pikmins are a threat. They'll smash your mash and hide in your shoes until you give them some grub. The Pikmins like to play peek-a-boo; you won't find them at first. If you squint twice and turn around you might just spot one there in the bread bin in amongst the Weetabix or nestled in the fridge. Larry is the worst-behaved one to worry about. You could find him in the biscuit tin, devouring all your digestives. So when you're eating your biscuits or mash always check there are no Pikmins nearby.

Isaac Durham (9)
Farsley Springbank Junior School, Farsley

Jeeper's Adventures

On Planet Fluffy World lived a fluffy cat called Jeepers. She liked to explore, so she wanted to visit Earth. She hopped in her rocket, flew past shooting stars, then landed on Earth. Jeepers saw there were lots of dogs.

"Oh no!" she cried. Jeepers hated dogs. She spotted a dog and used her Electro Cat Power on it.

The dog had spiky hair from the electricity! Then she realised it was Pummper from her own planet, disguised as a dog!

Jeepers said, "I'm sorry. Let's hop in the rocket and go home."

They said goodbye to Earth.

Aria Vargerson (9)

Farsley Springbank Junior School, Farsley

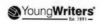

The Planet Fireport

Once, a girl named Poppy got kicked out of her family's home, as she had been a brat to her parents. What she didn't know was her family had set a magnificent, mesmerising portal to Planet Fireport.

This portal led her to a friendly but awfully dangerous monster named Marvin. He had long fangs in all three mouths, six eyes and a lemon-lime body. This planet was lush and loaded with monsters.

Marvin called Bob, his friend, to investigate her as he had never seen anything like her before. They had no idea what to do until...

Alice Lofthouse (9)

Farsley Springbank Junior School, Farsley

The Violet Moon

Once, there was a kind girl called Violet. However, a mean boy at school had taken the sparkle from her eyes and made her unhappy.

One day, something incredible began to happen! She turned into a huge monster with eight googly eyes, four chunky legs and one fluffy tail. The schoolchildren were petrified of the monster she had become! Violet knew that to break the spell, she had to pray to the violet moon.

That night, Violet prayed to break the curse. She did it! The sparkle returned to her eyes and the boy was never mean to her again.

Ava Lilley (8)

Farsley Springbank Junior School, Farsley

The Sea Snake

Then I saw it. However, I didn't exactly see it. It was all a blur. The ocean stirred and my ship rocked.

Early the next morning, the ocean stirred again, and in the middle was some sort of snake. It was the same colour as the ocean and it circled my ship - round and round and round.

Suddenly, it shot up from the ocean and started to attack me and my crew. The 'snake' was long and fierce. It didn't succumb, even if it was hit with a cannon.

The creature's tail swung up... My ship snapped in half!

Amelia Wilcock (10)

Farsley Springbank Junior School, Farsley

Finding A Family

It was a cold winter day with snow on the ground. Hedge and Hodge were cold, hungry and completely lost. They had no home and only had each other for company. They found shelter from the snowstorm underneath a little bush. All hope seemed lost as they struggled to stay warm until they heard children laughing. Harry and Elizabeth saw Hedge and Hodge and decided to rescue them. They placed them in a box full of straw and took them into the house to warm up. Hedge and Hodge were happy hedgehogs now that they had found a loving home.

Elizabeth Grace Carter (8)
Farsley Springbank Junior School, Farsley

Untitled

The waves of the ocean swung side to side, patiently tugging at the boat. Suddenly, something caught my eye in the depths of the blue ocean. The 'thing' came jumping up at me with its gagged shark-like teeth, but I pulled the engine before it could get me. I saw it; its face was narrow, and its disc-like eyes bulged out at me. As soon as I reached land and before I could run, I looked back and saw its repugnant tentacles rising from the water, uncovering its owl-like features. I stood there, my feet glued to the ground.

Bethany Todd (11)
Farsley Springbank Junior School, Farsley

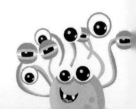

Life In Dog Land

Once upon a time, in the land of dogs, there lived a creature called Winners. He had orange wings and blue talons. He also had orange fur with blue spots on the edge. Even though he looked like this, he got bullied by dogs.

One day, a little girl called Stacey, who wore an orange jumper with blue spots on the sleeves, saw Winners. When Winners saw Stacey and Stacey saw Winners they knew they would be friends for life and never be bullied ever again. Together, they helped everyone in Dog Land to be happy and live a good life.

Samuel Wicks (8)
Farsley Springbank Junior School, Farsley

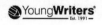

Jelly Joe

A creature lurks in the darkness. Not a human. Not an animal. An alien from the freezing planet of Neptune.

Compared to other creatures, this one stands out the most. Its stupendous figure has eight legs, three horns, five eyes and hundreds of venomous teeth. However, behind all of these frightening features is a generous, warmhearted monster.

All he ever wanted was a friend. No matter how nice he is, the children of Earth fear him the most. He feels really sad that no one is his friend, except for one human.

Seth Woodside (9)

Farsley Springbank Junior School, Farsley

Ballet From Beyond

Yesterday, I was going into the garden when I noticed something different: a large hole in the ground. I peered inside to find a small, chubby grey alien with a pink tutu on. It had one bright blue eye and two green antennae. When my brother found out, he wanted to keep it, though even the pet shop didn't know what it was but they did say the colour meant it was from Jupiter!

To this day, we still wonder why and how it got here but, for now, I'll keep it in my brother's bed and feed it teachers.

Tilly Davies (10)
Farsley Springbank Junior School, Farsley

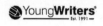

Banana Split

A green pineapple was on the beach until one day an asteroid came down and the pineapple came to life. It ran off and met a big, blue banana. They became great friends and ran into a desert. Banana and Pineapple got so hot then, unexpectedly, Banana peeled. Pineapple saw her naked! They ran back into the jungle and climbed a tree. As they listened to the sounds the animals made, they heard a monkey. It was getting closer and closer and then Banana was swept off her feet. It was a purple monkey. Banana was gone.

Alfie Winters (9)

Farsley Springbank Junior School, Farsley

King Bobo And His Colour-Changing Tears

King Bobo from Royal Creature Land wants to play football but his enemy, Queen Dodo, will not let him play. This makes him sad and cry lots of blue tears.

He plays football when Queen Dodo is asleep. When he plays football, his tears turn yellow and his frown turns upside down because he is so happy.

Queen Dodo realises that he is upset and lets him play. He joins a club. He is number ten, and a striker.

He scores lots of goals and he wins a trophy for being the top goal scorer. He is so happy.

Elliot Samuels (8)
Farsley Springbank Junior School, Farsley

The Lost Crocodile

Once there was a crocodile named Freddy. He had no friends so he decided he was going to go on a big adventure to try to find some friends. He got ready and started to sail to the deep sea. It was getting dark but he didn't give up, he was a little scared on the way but he was too brave. It was early in the morning and starting to get lighter again and he wasn't that scared now. It was lunch, he nearly gave up but then... he found friends, Lottie, Ben and Peter. They now have a BFF!

Emily Housley (7)
Farsley Springbank Junior School, Farsley

The Beany Boy

Once upon a time, there was a creature called Beany. He was born in a sewer and lived there for his whole life. But one day, he got found by a pea and a piece of broccoli. They put him in a blue tin that said Heinz Beans. It was freezing cold and hard. His friends and family, cousins and grandparents and he got thrown into a freezer with broken glass and icicles.
Later, a dad called David picked him up and threw him into his trolley. Then they went home and Beany got eaten for dinner.

Zack Habib (9)
Farsley Springbank Junior School, Farsley

77

The Adventure Of Beepdop

Once upon a time, in the deep dark universe of space, there was an alien in his big, green rocket. He was on his way to Mars for food but suddenly he crashed. Two hours later, he saw his spaceship broken. Then he heard shouting and people running. He started floating away. He noticed a shiny object in a bush and he dove in. He heard footsteps and quickly floated to his rocket. Then he used the object to fix his ship and shot off into space!

Prudence McGarry (10)
Farsley Springbank Junior School, Farsley

They Live Among Us

I froze in my seat, not believing my eyes. In front of me stood not one but two crazy creatures, no bigger than my little brother. One green, one yellow. I think the yellow one might be a girl. It had a flower growing from its head. They both had curly feet, fangs, and the biggest googly eyes I've ever seen. They made no sound. I rubbed my eyes, and they disappeared. Did I imagine them, or are there crazy creatures living among us?

Quorra Downing (9)

Farsley Springbank Junior School, Farsley

Lucy The Tricker

Once upon a time, Lucy tricked some creatures that were good into destroying their village. Then she brought them to the bad village to teach them to be bad so all of the creatures could be bad. So today, all creatures are mean and bad.

Luna Moore (7)
Farsley Springbank Junior School, Farsley

Helpful Bob

One day, there was an alien called Bob. He was two and he was going to preschool. His bag was all packed and ready to go. His mother told him to be polite. Bob took his mother's advice seriously. It was art, Bob's favourite subject, but someone wasn't kind to him and they kept on being unkind so Bob thought he would tell someone. It was scary but he did it and it was alright. Another person was having the same problem so Bob helped her know what to do and she told a teacher. No one was bullied again.

Timily Cripps (7)
Freeland CE Primary School, Freeland

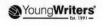

Bobetta's Dramatic Story

Once upon a time, there was a Nakid Pinacor who never went outside.

"Bobetta, come outside. There's nothing to worry about."

"Yes, there is. The trees," answered Bobetta.

Bobetta never went outside until, one day, she thought there was nothing to fear. She leaned back and started rolling across the big, juicy, furry grass.

"Oh my skibidy!" said Bobettaa. "I'm doing it. I'm so happy. LOL."

All of Bobetta's friends were so happy for her, until she got hit by a tornado and ended up in ICU. LOL. Luckily she made it out alive.

Ayla Hawgood (10)
Grouville Primary School, Grouville

Behind The Rainstone Waterfall

"Come on!" Nomi called.

Luna, Nomi's friend, caught up and the waterfall was just ahead. They cantered up the path to the sparkling waterfall and gazed at it.

"Wow!" Luna marvelled at the sight.

The friends jumped into the waterfall. They were stardust horses so it was no problem for them. Behind the waterfall was a collection of gems. They were stunned. The gems sparkled in the light and they were all different colours from black to light blue. Luna and Nomi were incredibly happy with their find. They couldn't help but feel proud. This was a great day!

Alanis McCarroll (11)
Grouville Primary School, Grouville

The Arkalope

The Arkalope is a skeletal moose covered in moss that wears a cow skull on its head and stands on two feet that crush anything in their path.
The Arkalope wanders inside the dark forest waiting for someone foolish to come wandering by. One day, a foolish monster hunter, armed with only a gun, came in search of the wondrous creature.
After a while, he came upon a ginormous cave.
"This is it," he gulped before proceeding into the cave.
It was pitch black, but before he could turn on his torch, he heard an earth-shattering screech.
Then...

Ned Monahan (11)

Grouville Primary School, Grouville

The Tales Of Marshmallow And Mocha: Woodland Brook

One rainy evening in Woodland Brook, Marshmallow wanted to go and explore. But Mocha wanted to stay and guard the den. Marshmallow set off on her journey.
A couple of hours passed and Marshmallow still wasn't home. Consequently, Mocha was starting to get worried, as it was dark now. Mocha then started to hunt for Marshmallow. Finally, Mocha found Marshmallow under an apple tree. Marshmallow was surprised to see Mocha, as he was going to protect the den.
Mocha told Marshmallow how it was dangerous to be out at this time. Then they both walked home.

Erin Troy (11)
Grouville Primary School, Grouville

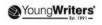

Untitled

Once upon a time, there was a family of Oogalies. They would eat children if they did not eat their potatoes. Oog was a happy Oogalie. He did not want to eat children; he wanted to dig for potatoes. Once, Oog was digging up potatoes, and he found lots of money. Being the Oogalie that he was, he had no idea what money was.

Oog questioned, "What is this?"

Oog was about to go home when he got hungry and ate all the money.

"Yum, yum, yum," said a happy Oog.

Oog ran home, asking himself, "What will I find tomorrow?"

Noah Monahan (11) & Buddy Sharkey (10)
Grouville Primary School, Grouville

Poke Spikes

One day there lived a little hedgehog called Prickly. Prickly had a special ability, not only could he shoot out spikes but sensed the weather or danger. The hedgehog went into the forest and got attacked and his spikes turned black. His spikes were in dark form and shot the predator with his dark spikes. Prickly had eighteen other different types of spikes. One day it was so hot that his spikes turned red for fire because of the weather, but his family loved him and he loved them as well, no matter how dangerous his spikes were they still loved him.

Jake Kelly (10)
Grouville Primary School, Grouville

Chunky John And Lanky Joe And The Mine

Once there were two old creatures called Chunky John and Lanky Joe. They worked in a small mine which was under the soaring mountains.

One day on the weekend, they decided to go down the mine to explore hidden parts that were blocked off. When they went down there, they saw the blocked passage and went to check it out. Lanky Joe went to one side and Chunky John went to the other. Lanky Joe found a lever and pulled it and it opened. Inside were sparkling diamonds and emeralds. They shouted, "We're going to be rich!"

William Austin (11) & Saul Brennan (11)

Grouville Primary School, Grouville

The Golden Eggs

One day there was a nice monster, Ned. Ned was bored at home until his mum told him to go to the store and get golden eggs. Ned was confused; he had never heard of the idea of golden eggs.
"At the human store, go get them," Mum asked.
Ned reluctantly agreed, still having zero clue what golden eggs were. He got into his space pod and hid his alien features, and he started the search. After an hour, even the employees were concerned, but finally he found it. His mum meant the brand Golden Eggs, not the real thing!

Daisy Campbell
Grouville Primary School, Grouville

The Aggressive Story Of Saffy And Timmy

Once there was a strange-looking turtle called Saffy. Saffy was swimming in the ocean one day when she came across a dinosaur named Timmy, one that swam around in the ocean deep. She feared this underwater creature at first, but she ended up becoming friends with this dinosaur. Every day they would meet up and talk about their lives etc. They had been meeting up for at least a whole month and they were best friends. One day Saffy was extremely hungry, so she decided to inhale and eat Timmy, very aggressively she fed him to herself.

Nina Mousdale (11)

Grouville Primary School, Grouville

Grass And Lawnmower

Once upon a time, a grass wanted friends but she didn't have any friends so she set out to find some. Off she went, she found some friends but they weren't hers, Libe, Rock, Flower, Tree and Wheat, none of them wanted to be her friend until she saw the lawnmower. She went up to him and he started chasing her until she hid and then jumped out into the lawnmower engine, the grass got snipped into pieces, but she managed to turn the lawnmower off. Over years and years, that grass turned that garden into a beautiful paradise.

Lyra McKeown (11)
Grouville Primary School, Grouville

The Weird Capybara And Horsasaurus

One day there was a horse named Neeyah, and she was trotting along on her hairy little feet on the hairy air on a little patch of grass. She was only used to seeing hairy grass and prickly water, no other animals and normal things like her, until she was trotting along on soft water. Then started to walk on non-hairy grass until she saw a dinosaur named Grippy and they got combined into a Horsasaurus! But then there was a very hungry Capybara who decided to eat the Horsasaurus feet and their very cool shoes.

Indie Roberts (10)

Grouville Primary School, Grouville

Porky Pig

Once there was a pig named Porky. He absolutely loved playing in mud and his best friend was a seagull named Gully. Sometimes when it is too hot and the mud is not wet they liked to dig in the dirt. One day when they were digging they came across a dinosaur fossil! They were amazed at their discovery. Gully pulled it out of the ground and they both inspected it. Porky tapped it twice with his hoof and it came to life! They all became best friends and they were the best trio in the world.

Maddison de Loynes (10)
Grouville Primary School, Grouville

93

Mabel Never Gave Up

Once, there was a caterpillar called Mabel. She was always made fun of for being small and scary. She had five eyes and no hands because of her big, sharp teeth, but that did not stop her from doing stuff that she liked, like surfing and going on bike rides with her mum. She did not have many friends, but she never stopped believing in herself. Because of that, she became the most beautiful butterfly ever. She was on TV and was the most famous creature ever because she never doubted herself.

Mae Jackson (10)
Grouville Primary School, Grouville

KFC Is The Best

Once, there was an unbelievably strong football team in the Fast Food Cup that was smashing Farmer McDonald 101-0. Their name was KFC (Kraken Friceled Chips). They beat King Burger 16-2 in their next game. Meanwhile, in Europe, BIFA had made a team that some people called invincible. Surely they were going to beat KFC. Their star player was Sloppy J, the Cyclops, and they were called Chick-Fil-Your-Stomach. The game started, and zap, the world was shocked. The final score was 40-1 for KFC!

Henry Skrivelis (11) & Finley Norbury (11)
Grouville Primary School, Grouville

The Oogway Chronicles

Once upon a time, there were two best friends. They both became generals together.

One day they found a hidden panda tribe. Oogway asked the pandas to teach him the power of chi, except Kai wanted all the powers for himself. He tried to kill all the pandas to sell their chi. Oogway was not going to let that happen so they battled for two days non-stop. Their fight shook the earth until Oogway trapped them both in the spirit world where they would fight for the rest of eternity.

Noah Camara

Grouville Primary School, Grouville

Untitled

Once there was a creature Goku. Goku went to the beach to play. While he was there, Goku went underwater and came across a rock. He explored it. As he was exploring, a piece fell off. He found a chest. He opened it and found a letter and a toy, saying: 'He does not exist he does not exist'.
Goku was shocked. When he looked at the toy a big creature emerged from the dark. It chased him. When he looked around it was gone.
He got home and it had all ended.

Andre Camacho (11)
Grouville Primary School, Grouville

Jeffery's Mysterious Story

Once upon a time, there was a little monster that was called Jeffery and he lived in a small house. The house was near a beach and he would love to play all day on it. One day he found an alien spaceship, so he went inside and was in outer space. He asked the green squishy alien if he could stay and they said yes. So he found some things to play with, but it was time to go home. When he got home he told his parents. They were so surprised, then he went to sleep!

Eva De Castro (10) & Amelia Linstead (10)

Grouville Primary School, Grouville

Cranky Creatures

One day, I was in the zoo and I was in the flamingo enclosure. I noticed a few bugs, they started to crawl up my leg. I flicked them off me so fast I felt a tooth chip off. I ran away as the zookeeper chased after me. After the zookeeper caught up to me and asked me what was wrong, I explained and she said that is what insects like to do, so I calmed down a little bit more and took a sip of water. Shortly after, my day was ended.

Charlotte Wiltcher Woodman (11)
Grouville Primary School, Grouville

Cray Cray Monsters

Once upon a time, there was a ladybug named Steve! He lived in the jungle and he loved exploring it. One day, he found an abandoned plane. He searched the plane and found a secret room in the back of the plane. It was filled with money. He went back home and told his parents. His parents had followed him to the plane. Steve showed his parents who were in total shock. His mum screamed, "We are rich!"

Nina Kordzinska (11)
Grouville Primary School, Grouville

Luna Moonlight And The Crazy Flying Hedgehog

Luna Midnight was born to Draco and Lily Moonlight on the 27th of June 2022. She had a best friend called Neville who was a flying hedgehog, who was crazy! Luna is two and Neville is three. They go to the nursery together. Their nursery was called Magic Faraway Tree, the best school ever in Neville and Luna's opinion! Neville and Luna went to the beach with Lily and Draco because it was a nice sunny day.

Maiyah-Sophie Misson (11)
Grouville Primary School, Grouville

The Infinity Space Monster

Once at Heartford on a late night, the moon was out, the wolves were howling, and out of the cupboard, a monster appeared.

The next day a teacher came to grab something but... "Raw" the monster came out and the teacher was dead!

But then the children came in storming to the cupboard, there was a big bang and the monster and one child were gone.

The monster had teleported.

"I'm Magpie," said the monster.

"I'm Alex," said the child. "Can we be friends?"

"Of course," said Magpie.

"Oh wait, I'm going to be late."

Lily M (8)
Hertford Junior School, Hollingdean

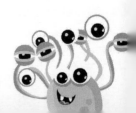

Billybob Falls In Love

Once upon a time, there was a three-eyed monster called Billybob and he lived in Crazy Creature City. In school, he got bullied a lot but one day he skipped school and went for a walk in the forest. He came out to find a new city. He found a three-eyed monster and her name was Bella. They quickly fell in love and had children and made a population of three-eyed monsters. They all lived happily ever after.

But, in the future, they are lurking around somewhere maybe hidden in the bushes.

Leah D (10)
Hertford Junior School, Hollingdean

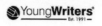
Space Kitties

"Three, two, one... blast-off!"
I was in a rocket on my way to explore a new planet. I had wanted to for aeons! I was soaring through space and soon Earth was just a tiny marble in the blank, black room.
Many years later, we landed on a dusty, red planet. "I'm on Mars!" I exclaimed. I slipped down the shuttle's ladder and onto the planet's surface. Unexpectedly, loads of adorable kitten-like creatures popped out of some craters. "Aww!" I sighed before they suddenly bared their teeth and attacked with very vicious expressions on their faces.

Hannah Farrell (9)
Ivy House School, Golders Green

The Joy Of Being Evil

Just another day of destroying someone's classroom, I thought, emptying out the ruler tray. The Evil Centre for Evil Beings would be so proud of me. I was crushing this new job! The door was opening. I had to hide.

"Look what the furry green monster with twenty-five eyes that has elastic arms has done to our classroom," exclaimed a girl in the class.

I suddenly felt something sad inside of me. Guilt? At that moment I felt so sad I stepped out of my hiding spot, apologised to them and surprisingly they forgave me. I'm a good being now.

Alanna Ramchandani (9)

Ivy House School, Golders Green

The Deadly Beast

Today is the day I can go out and drink all the delicious blood of those pesky humans!
First, I decide to head to the princess's palace; I deserve the very best! I can steal all of those shiny jewels and maybe even the vicious guards. They look tasty!
I head towards the palace and find the princess. She doesn't look the same as she usually does. She's wearing a red and black dress, skull earrings and a black cloak.
I'm impressed, so I enter the Royal Hall and join her as her pet partner in crime!

Vanessa Edde (10)
Ivy House School, Golders Green

Nowhere To Run

It had got out. I could feel my heart thumping, thumping louder than the screams around me. I felt like I wanted to exit out of this ruined world. I was terrified. But I didn't have a choice. The whole world was depending on me to save their existence. I had to stop the dreaded Ursa and imprison it on Planet Furbo. Suddenly, I snapped back, and I could feel the hot air of the Ursa right above me, its eyes staring into my soul. I couldn't be afraid now. I grabbed his neck and... *whoosh!* Back to Planet Furbo...

Arina Nemodruk (10)
Ivy House School, Golders Green

Exile

I had been exiled from my planet to spend the rest of my days here on Earth, thinking about what I had done. I was scavenging in my usual place, the dump. I was peering in, when I felt hands grab onto me like a toy. The hands threw me onto the conveyor belt. Without a doubt, I was done for. I had never been so scared in my life!

"Eek!" I squealed and the hands came back, reached in and lifted me to safety. The old feeling came back. The reason I'd been exiled. I violently attacked him.

Lavinia Marsh (9)
Ivy House School, Golders Green

The New 'Pet'

"Wake up!" shouted Ethan. Zephus's horns were covered in blood, and venomous acid circled around his piercing fangs.

"I'm awake!" screeched Zephus in a demonic tone.

"That gives me goosebumps," mumbled Ethan.

Zephus was a three-year-old creature from Mars. When Ethan was eleven, he had always wanted a pet, so his parents went to a pet store and they found Zephus.

Once, Zephus told Ethan a secret and Ethan's parents weren't happy. Then, one night, Ethan woke up.

"Zephus, go to sleep!" shouted Ethan.

The next day he asked, "Zephus, where are you? What is that noise?"

Briken Mia (10)
James Cambell Primary School, Dagenham

Fruit Or Veggie?

Once there was a planet called Planet Veggie. In it roamed fruits and veggies, the enemies. One day, Waterwinda Watermelon met her friend Tomato. No one knew if he was a fruit or veggie. Just then, Waterminda saw her deadliest enemy, Carrot. He started, "Tomato is a veggie!"

"No fruit!" Waterminda demanded.

A war had begun. Waterminda wrapped her hands, and vines, around Carrot and strangled him. Suddenly Carrot twirled so fast that he escaped from her. Then, he spat sticky roots at Waterminda.

"Stop fighting! I forgot to tell you that I'm both. Fruit and veggie," interrupted Tomato innocently.

Maisha Hussain (11)

James Cambell Primary School, Dagenham

Magical Creatures Go On An Adventure

In La La Land, Lulu is a girl full of curiosity. Lulu is seen flying to Earth for a mission. Lulu eagerly gets transported to Earth.

"The scenery looks so beautiful," Lulu says with an awestruck look.

Instantaneously, a human appears, looking furious at Lulu. She decides to ignore it, but the human has taken the precious dazzling crystal.

"Stop! Stop there, I need that!" shouts Lulu, floating.

Lulu furiously snatches the dazzling crystal. Lulu's sister comes to the rescue and holds Lulu and the crystal. Now Lulu and her sister are back in La La Land and live happily ever after.

Hephzibah Adedayo (10)
James Cambell Primary School, Dagenham

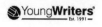

Will Mr Frustrate Ever Be Happy?

Angrily, Mr Frustrate had been pouting about his lost money. Everyone knew to leave Mr Frustrate when he was angry, except Mrs Joyful. Many attempts were made to turn that gloomy frown upside down, yet Mr Frustrate remained angry. So, Mrs Joyful hit him with her special happy dust! Oh no, that wasn't happy dust; that was super, mega, extreme, angry, angry, angry dust! What has Mrs Joyful done?

"Everyone, remain calm. I'm kidding, run!"

Mr Frustrate was now Mr Super, Mega, Extreme, Angry, Angry, Angry Frustrate. If even Mrs Joyful can't make him happy, who can? What will she attempt next?

Jannah Hossain (10)
James Cambell Primary School, Dagenham

Zeema's Secret

In the heart of the jungle, there lived a creature. Its name was Zeema, whispered only by the bravest souls around campfires.

Zeema was no ordinary monster; it was a weaver of nightmares. Each night it emerged from the roots, its eyes like shimmering rubies.

Its body was a patchwork of moss and bark, limbs elongated and twisted. Zeema fed on fear, lurking near the village, listening to the children's stories.

One night, a curious child named Amelia wandered into the jungle. She stumbled upon Zeema, who watched her with hunger. But, instead of screaming, she whispered, "I know your secret."

Aarya Bancey (11)
James Cambell Primary School, Dagenham

Fuggler Island

"People. Tonight we will destroy Fuggler Island!"
With complete panic, Steve ran to the rescue.
Jumping over tall buildings and sliding under tight
spaces, Steve would win.

They were running towards Fuggler Island with
sticks and matches. "Burn it, burn it!" Steve got
hold of a rope and swung from one to two, he built
up the courage to snatch the matches and burn
their hair on fire!

"Argh, my head! That's why you don't mess with
us," muffled Steve. He had done it. He saved
Fuggler Island. Maybe humans will live there one
day. Who knows because I don't.

Holly Wingate (10)

James Cambell Primary School, Dagenham

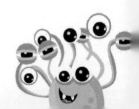

Dojo Land In Dojonica's Eyes

In Dojo Kingdom, there was a little girl who was bullied for her size. Despite being a princess, her parents only favoured her beautiful, skinny siblings. They'd call her names and laugh without guilt whilst ignoring her feelings.

One day, she got sick. During that time, she lost a lot of weight, which led to her parents caring for her so she'd keep full.

Her mood enlarged. She always had an extraordinary look on her face from then onwards, and was very happy.

And that's the tale of what Princess Dojonica once experienced in her mysterious life that continues forever.

Zeenat Adeniran (10)

James Cambell Primary School, Dagenham

The Young Pear

The young pear cautiously walked into the forest. She knew it was forbidden. But she continued and she arrived at the barrier of vegetables and fruits. Her face filled with shock when she saw a... vegetable!

She was never allowed to see one but she asked it, "What are you?"

The vegetable looked at her and then finally said, "I'm a broccoli." Then Pear straight away knew what they both wanted, the flower. Not long after they saw it... They both looked at each other, then ran to the tree. At last, they looked at each other and they both grabbed it...

Ellie-Mae Sullivan (10)

James Cambell Primary School, Dagenham

The Man And The Robotic Monster

Many years after Earth was invaded, a man lived with his son, Ami, on Mars. Times were tough - the man's wife died and a few years later Ami died. The man had felt pain ever since. He tried thinking but nothing came until the man figured out a brilliant idea.

He built a robot clone of his son. He trained it to do everything his son could. Everything turned out fine until... The boy robot 'drank' water and malfunctioned himself, causing him to achieve immense powers. He could shape-shift and destroy structures. Sadly, the boy became sinful and destroyed Mars.

Yusef Ali (10)
James Cambell Primary School, Dagenham

Untitled

In the undergrowth in the land of potatoes, there was one particular monster who grew into Potmas and that's where the monsters started. Some grew wonky, some scary looking.

This all happened on our farm, in the field, there were lots of shrubs, bushes and trees where the monsters started. Potmas was a horrible potato, he would throw potatoes at the other monsters and they would be hurt but he did not care.

One day Potmas threw too many potatoes. He flooded the whole town. Before the monsters could get a chance they all shouted at Potmas and waddled away.

Millie Soane (11)

James Cambell Primary School, Dagenham

Fug's Adventure

In a cosy bedroom, Fug The Fuggler doll lay still on the shelf, dreaming of adventure.

One night, as the moon peeked through the curtains Fug felt a gentle tug. It was Sparkle, the mischievous fairy doll, inviting Fug on a magical journey. With a nod Fug jumped down, his button eyes shining with excitement. Together they flew on a paper aeroplane through the starry sky, landing in a candy kingdom. They danced with gummy bears and slid down rainbow slides until dawn painted the horizon. As the sun rose, Fug returned home, his heart brimming with tales of wonder.

Lily Gladman (11)
James Cambell Primary School, Dagenham

119

Left In The Desert

Once in the Galaxy of Stars, a young alien called Acheron flew in her spaceship. Her controls were broken and consequently, she crashed on Earth. Acheron fell into Mr Smith's backgarden. He saw her and wondered. Acheron went into the house and drew eleven cats. Mr Smith's friends understood that it was fuel for her spaceship. They went to get the cats. As a reward, Acheron allowed them to get into the spaceship. In a flash of light, they were in a desert. When they got out Acheron waved goodbye and went. As for Mr Smith and his friends, they were left.

Shakina Boodhoo (11)

James Cambell Primary School, Dagenham

The Slay Of His Ememy

On Tuesday, there was a crazy creature called Brian and he was getting dressed for another day at school. He was on his way to school and he was worried about his family because he had an enemy. He arrived at school and he was still scared. His enemy was sitting next to him. "What are you doing...?" The bell rang and school had finished.

When he got back from school, "Oh no, my parents are not here." He was trying to find his siblings and parents when he saw his enemy and he got stopped. He was slaying. His family were saved.

Bilal Brika (10)

James Cambell Primary School, Dagenham

The Dragon Killer

On Earth, there is a giant dragon who steals treasure and precious gems, kidnaps children and feasts on their flesh.

As the dragon tries to consume a girl, she runs away. Suddenly, a silence fills the air. Then, in the distance, a person called Titular - the hero - leaps into the air with a giant sword. He wields it to bring justice and vengeance to all the children who have been devoured by the dragon.

The hero strikes the beast. Defeated, it lies down. The hero wins and he lays his sword down. All the people cheer, "Hooray, hooray!"

Leonel Syla (11)

James Cambell Primary School, Dagenham

The Midnight Snack

"Squeak!"

"Fluff, what is it now?" The animal's eyes glared at the girl. She looked at the creature with eyes filled with hope on her bed. "Fine, just this once but promise me you will be quiet?" asked Mia, showing sympathy. The animal then did the tiniest squeak that not even a mouse could do. Licking its lips, the creature rushed out of Mia's bed to the door. As Mia opened the door her eyes peered out like a hawk, trying to spot any sign of her mother. "Okay, the coast is clear." The animal rushed out...

Eve Ellis (11)
James Cambell Primary School, Dagenham

The Nighthowl

The Nighthowl standing at an imposing eight feet tall, this fearsome beast has piercing red eyes that glow ominously in the shadows. Its body covered in slick, black fur, seem to absorb the light around it. Nearly invisible in the darkness, The Nighthowl possesses unnaturally long limbs each ending in razor-sharp claws capable of slicing through steel as if it were paper. Its jaws are wide and filled with rows of jagged teeth, dripping with venom that paralyses its prey. The Nighthowl is not just a predator; it is an embodiment of night terrors lurking.

Michelle Thompson (11)

James Cambell Primary School, Dagenham

How Fiomba Saved His World!

Once, Fiomba was going on a trip to the forest of Fiomlas. While he explored the forest, he saw a water goomba!
What was it doing there? Why was it there? And how had it got there? As Fiomba went to investigate, he couldn't believe his eyes! They were creating more water goombas.
Fiomba ran to ask why they were there and was told their UFO had broken and landed there. They needed more of their kind to fix it.
After a while, everything was fixed and the water goombas left. Fiomba turned the remaining water goombas back to normal.

Ramina Gawau (10)
James Cambell Primary School, Dagenham

Sockie The Sock Thief

As the sun began to set, Sockie's invisibility had worn off. Sophie prepared for bed. She was exhausted as she brushed her teeth and removed her socks. She staggered into bed and within minutes she was snoring.

Suddenly, Sockie noticed a pair of pink fluffy socks on the floor next to him. He mischievously swiped them under Sophie's bed where he resides at night-time trying not to get caught. He gave a gentle sniff to make sure they were not smelly, as he hated nothing more. As the sun began to rise, he quickly returned to Sockville.

Mia Barclay (11)

James Cambell Primary School, Dagenham

My Crazy Creature!

I stumbled upon a strange creature in the forest. It had the head of a lion, the body of a snake and the wings of a bird. I couldn't believe my eyes. I cautiously approached it, but to my surprise, it started to speak. "Hello there, human. I am a magical creature created by a wizard. My name is Chimera, and I can grant you three wishes." I couldn't believe my luck. I quickly made my wishes, and Chimera disappeared, leaving me in awe of my crazy encounter. From that day onwards, I always believed in the magic of the forest.

Olivia Umeh (9)
James Cambell Primary School, Dagenham

The Horrifying Nightmares

One night, when I was asleep, I saw a creature that had never been seen before. It had a demon power, which was terrifying, so I tried to escape from this nightmare.

I thought it was trying to kill me, but it couldn't happen because I had hidden powers. He really thought he was the only one with powers.

He tried several times to fight me, but couldn't hurt me. He had a friend called Creepy Crybaby, but little did he know I had my strongest friend: Demon Dare. Then I and my friend killed them both.

They wondered how.

Kapilan Ketheeswaran (11)

James Cambell Primary School, Dagenham

Rubies

On a small planet called Exbeplamt, a boy hid two rubies. Whoever found them would be known as the best monster ever. Gooblexb was confident because of his wit, but Gib'bb was also exceptionally smart. The horn blew; it was time. Everyone ran. Gooblexb checked the mountain, and he saw a mysterious red glow, but in the distance, he saw Gib'bb dashing toward the ruby. Gooblexb ran to the mountain but saw a different ruby. When Gooblexb came out, Gib'bb had a ruby. Gooblexb jumped on Gib'bb and took the ruby. Gooblexb won.

Baalis Odofin (10)
James Cambell Primary School, Dagenham

129

Rainbow Culture

Once there lived a creature called Rainbow who was very lonely. But one day she decided to make a bunch of rainbow planets to get friends. But she did not know what would happen.

After creating all the planets everybody started to follow her around. It got annoying so to fix the issue Rainbow fused all of the rainbow planets and rainbow people into a mega rainbow planet. All of the people became one big friend to Rainbow. Rainbow was extremely happy to finally have friends. Rainbow hopes to have friends for her whole entire life.

Ryan Cole (10)
James Cambell Primary School, Dagenham

It Will Be Okay

Bob, the smelly, three-eyed, fluffy and very weird monster, sat there all alone in the noisy, never-ending playground. He had no friends. He felt hopeless.

Bob wondered if he should run far away or maybe talk to his teacher, Miss Bowness.

All of a sudden, Miss Bowness came up to him and told him that, if there was anything he was worrying about, he should speak to her, so he seized the chance to express how he felt.

He explained that he had nobody to play with. Miss Bowness said he could play with the Year 5s instead.

Evie-Mae Sutton (10)
James Cambell Primary School, Dagenham

131

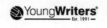

The Leprechaun And The Brits

Once, there were two kids who went on a vacation to Ireland for Saint Patrick's Day. They landed at Dublin airport and then saw a rainbow. They kept walking and found the end of the rainbow with a pot of gold and a leprechaun who was sleeping. They stole the gold and dashed away from the scene, they went to Galway and they saw that same leprechaun and he was mad! They ran away in fear and dashed to Achill. They kept running and running and they were scared, their souls left their bodies and saw the leprechaun flying in the air.

Shah-Aayan Ahmed (10)

James Cambell Primary School, Dagenham

Wiggly Saves The Day

Wiggly is a monster with lots of friends in Fun Town, he loves hugs but has one enemy, Slappy. One day, Slappy invaded Fun Town and captured all of Wiggle's friends. He took over the town, so Wiggly had to save the day. What could he do? He decided that he would transform into Huggy. When Wiggly found Slappy he saw his dog Scruffy, his only family. Suddenly he became the Super Red Monster Huggy. He fired a power beam obliterating Slappy! Saving his friends and family. To celebrate he had an amazing party. The end, or is it?

Charlie Tyler (10)
James Cambell Primary School, Dagenham

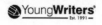
New School

Difrancea was joining her new school and about to step into her classroom. As she stepped in she started receiving rude comments. At this point, she had no expectations of making friends.

A week passed by and she started getting bullied because of her appearance.

"Freak, ugly," all of the comments got to her. She stood up for herself and turned into a powerful creature.

"Do not talk to me like you know me!"

The head teacher walked in.

"Difrancea, my office now!"

Favour O-Oluwasemilore (11)

James Cambell Primary School, Dagenham

Winning Isn't All

One day, a monster called Penly was writing a book yet this was not his first time. He loved writing books and there was a competition in Popper Town and he signed up. Penly grabbed his pen and got to writing. But his tub of ink fell on his book, it was ruined. Penly's heart sank but he sent it off regardless. A few days later Penly got a letter, he had won the book competition. Penly jumped for joy, this proves to pursue your dreams no matter what. So if you ever feel sad just think of Penly, don't give up.

Henry Rayner (11)
James Cambell Primary School, Dagenham

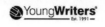

Lola's Adventure Home

Lola was moved from Jacuziworld at the age of three to London, but she moved with her grandma and she wanted to meet her baby sister who was only one month old and really missed the rest of her family. She started walking towards the car but on her way to Jacuziland, she came face to face with her enemy. She got out of her car and turned herself invisible; because it didn't work inside of anything. She made it there and she was so happy to see her parents and siblings, her sister was now seven and they played.

Isla Mursell (11)

James Cambell Primary School, Dagenham

The Story Of Bobasaurus, The Evil Monster

Once, there was a monster named Bobasaurus and he was abandoned by his evil parents in the middle of the creepy woods. He was miserable and had no hope, until one day he found a way out. When he got out he wanted revenge and started to destroy the city, until a superhero came along. He made his way to Bobasaurus and pushed him violently to the ground. Bobasaurus got up and unleashed all his anger in one punch and missed. He was shocked to have missed. Suddenly, he realised what he was doing was wrong and ran away.

Fraser McCarthy (11)
James Cambell Primary School, Dagenham

Zoge's Soup

There was a carrot named Zoge who was making carrot soup for the town. All of a sudden the fruit came in anger because the town was flooded with carrot soup. All of the vegetables had no idea what to do or say so they just started eating it all. One by one the fruit did as well but the fruit started to explode one by one, so the vegetables started to get worried. Eventually, they took a break and the carrot soup began to disappear. The vegetables were happy forever. They were overjoyed and ate soup.

Poppy Rawlinson (10)
James Cambell Primary School, Dagenham

Blep's Parents

Blep is an alien looking for his parents. He has looked everywhere for them for five years, and he's still looking for them.

He goes around, asking other aliens, and they say they don't know where his parents are until he hears his parents are on Earth!

He wants to build a rocket so he can bring them back, so he spends a year building and learning how to fly it.

He flies it to the Earth, finds them and looks for oil for the rocket ship. Then he finds some and goes home.

Castiel Trench
James Cambell Primary School, Dagenham

Lord 'N' Saviour

Once upon a time, there was a young, beautiful girl. One day, she got kidnapped! Twenty years passed and no one ever saved her until an ugly monster found her lying in her case.

Just as he went to kiss her, a wicked man took over and gave her a kiss, but there was still no sign of breath.

The ugly monster pushed him out of the way and gave her a humungous kiss, and she awoke from her slumber.

In the heat of the moment, she turned into a monster. They lived happily ever after.

Freya Ellis (10)
James Cambell Primary School, Dagenham

The Amazing Life Of Bob

Bob was a very innocent boy until the humans invaded. They had eaten all his friends, family and neighbours. He had to flee, as the humans were growing hungrier.

Later, he was the last one. They knew he was alive and the reward for getting him and bringing him to the king was one billion pounds.

After a year, the world was going feral over getting him, as the price had gone up to one trillion pounds.

As Bob was walking around, he encountered a human and started to run.

Ahmed Suleyman (10)
James Cambell Primary School, Dagenham

Untitled

One day on Planet Danger Teeny Tiny Terror was flying through his planet when he heard a thud. He looked around, confused, until he saw it. It was Big Bad Buster. He tried to fly away but he got grabbed and robbed of his moon cake. He was furious so he needed a plan for revenge.

He set up a trip that would trick Big Bad Buster. He had a table and a moon cake. As soon as Big Bag Buster grabs him, he will fall down a hole. But will Teeny Tiny Terror get the moon cake back?

Tyler Sims (11)

James Cambell Primary School, Dagenham

The Tale Of The Shifter Of Shapes

The Shifter Of Shapes. I stare at it amazed. No one knows where it came from. No one knows when it will leave but the only thing we know is it appeared from outer space. I watch it shift, it goes big then small like how a story unfolds.

Suddenly, it meets my gaze. We stare at each other for eternity then it shape-shifts away. That's the story of the Shifter of Shapes which has more than one hundred faces.

John Alogba (11)
James Cambell Primary School, Dagenham

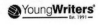
Monster Ark

I felt angry for losing to Superhero and I swore to get revenge on him but I didn't know what I could do. Nevermind. I could give him a bunch of crimes to solve. It will get the superhero overwhelmed and I will finally end him today. Haha time to test my new suit.

Akachuwku Onuorah (10)

James Cambell Primary School, Dagenham

The Scariest Day

One day, June was cheating with Google. He was so tired cheating that he accidentally typed 'shapy-breezy'. He saw facts about it and copied it. He dreamt of himself at home playing fourteen games all in one go. He played for a while, not knowing the iPad was Shapy-Breezy. Shapy-Breezy was getting tired, so he shape-shifted back to his normal self, letting June know. June chased after Shapy-Breezy and ran into a lamp post. An officer noticed the incident. So the officer called back-up and chased after the creature. The creature shape-shifted into a lamp post. Then, the silly creature ran away.

David Onyenwenu (8)
Rochester Riverside CE Primary School, Rochester

Blobby Unleashed

Once on Planet Slime a baby called Blobby was born. He had a moustache and was very kind. Ten years later... *Boom!* Planet Slime was about to explode. Blobby's parents did not know what to do so they shot their baby into space and to another planet. When Blobby landed he saw different types of babies had landed there too. *Is this happening everywhere?* he thought. When he landed he discovered teachers were making kids do boring homework. So he ate the teachers and homework and they had a party and invited other friendly, kind, funny and cool monsters.

Sofia Georgieva (7)
Rochester Riverside CE Primary School, Rochester

The Minnie Shop

In a big house there lived a girl called Sophie. One day she went with her mum to the Co-op. In the local shop, Shaggy the monster was lurking around. The girl said, "Where are the apples?" to her mum. Shaggy slowly went to find the apples. Then he saw the apples hiding, then he went to get one but Glass Man attacked, but Shaggy threw an apple at him. Then he went flying out of the window and Shaggy gave the apple to Sophie and she paid at the counter and walked home with the apple to eat it.

Matthew Sutch (7)

Rochester Riverside CE Primary School, Rochester

The Monster Who Became A Better Person

Sloppy was an extremely grumpy creature. He worked as a lost property man. He hated children but he was so grumpy he couldn't find another job! Then, one day, he found an orange T-shirt. He liked it so much he took it home to wear it. When he was done with it, he put it in his cupboard. The next day it was gone! So he went to lots of other lost property places, but they were horrible, just like him. He decided to become a better person. The T-shirt was actually in the toilet!

Reese Agoro (8)

Rochester Riverside CE Primary School, Rochester

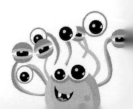

The Silly Monster

Dunnu saw a mysterious box on the pathway so jumped to see what was inside. After, he just sat on the box really scared because it was full of his enemy's pencils! He tried to get down but it was too late because he had already fallen down into water. He was scared but he noticed something. There was a tiny hole on the very bottom. He tried to swim to the side, but he went to the wrong side. He was so silly because he completely forgot about his awesome powers.

Noemi Astorri (8)
Rochester Riverside CE Primary School, Rochester

Dave The Drinker

One day after school, Lorcán was invited to a pub. Only he could see a monster called Dave. Lorcán ran to the bathroom and looked at the ceiling and saw loads of Daves. So he ran back to the bar. But the other Dave tried to bite him, again and again. Lorcán knew that Daves hate water. So, Lorcán got some water. Lorcán said to Dave, "Drink some." Then he lived with Lorcán forever.

Lorcàn Steele (7)
Rochester Riverside CE Primary School, Rochester

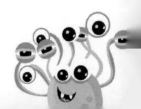

The Way Out Of School

One day Emma was in school playing outside, then the bell rang. She went inside for her history lesson. "This is boring," she said. A couple of minutes later she fell asleep. She dreamt of a monster.

When she woke up, she saw that same monster. It took away the teachers, it took away the school work. They disappeared into Emma's happy place. She was on the roller coaster. It was fun. She was happy.

Ismé Nkansah (8)
Rochester Riverside CE Primary School, Rochester

The Sweet Monster

The child made salad but Dad didn't like it. She went to bed.

The next day the child went to the wood and heard something. She turned, scared, there was a candy monster. Then she went towards Dad and Dad was so happy. The child and the monster were friends. They were friends so every night and day they had sweets every day.

Ruby Foster (7)
Rochester Riverside CE Primary School, Rochester

The Dream

"I'm tired," said Boogaly the creative creature, so he dozed off. "Ooh, wait, where am I?"

"You're in Oogaland Past!" said an unknown voice.

"Why?" Boogaly said.

"I don't know!" said the voice. "Oh, here comes your enemy!"

"Hi," said the enemy. "You sound familiar."

"Of course I sound familiar, I've been talking to you this whole time!"

"What? So who are you?"

"I am the Oogaland Lake Monster. So is this when we fight?" said Oogaland Lake Monster.

"I'm in a dream though," said Boogaly. "But we can't change the past. But!"

"No, but it is time. Goodbye."

Bronwyn McCabe (10)
St Peter's Primary School, Newry

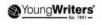

Ruby Vs Kevin

Once in the seas: "Where's the captain?" yelled
Max at the tip of the ship.

"She's in her office," said Jess.

Max walked over and knocked on the door and
said, "Come on."

"I'm coming." Ruby walked out.

Thump, thump, thump!

"What's that noise?" Suddenly Kevin the Kraken
slashed the ship in half. "Ha ha ha!" laughed Kevin.
Suddenly Ruby turned into a
bunny/demon/dragon/wolf. She jumped up in the
air and scratched Kevin's eyes and tentacles. Ruby
turned back into a person and said, "Do you want
to do that again?"

"No, please, no! Fine, you win!"

Lexi Kennedy (9)
St Peter's Primary School, Newry

Snakeeye Vs The Dragons

In Dragonville, far in the trees, a snake lives.
"I'm Snakeeye, I stay in the woods with the other snakes. The dragons took over Snakeville and we are trying to make a plan. But first, we have to get Snakeville back. There's a dragon at the entrance. If I hit him in the head, we should get inside Snakeville."
Bam!
"We are inside. Oh no, more dragons are coming."
I ran behind a tree.
A dragon said, "We want peace!"
I came out.
"You want peace?" I said.
"Yes," said a different dragon.
"Okay," I said.
We lived happily in peace.

Elisha Duffy (10)
St Peter's Primary School, Newry

155

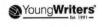
The Day I Had A Snowball Fight

"Neptune is amazing for snowball fights!" I shouted, after getting Master Kelp out.

"Wait a minute," Master said. "Why is it getting brighter? Uh-oh, the sun! It's coming out!" Master shouted. We ran back to the spacebus, geared up, then set off towards the sun.

"Three, two, one, charge!" The sun sent some minions to attack us. "Children, you fight the minions, I'll fight the big one."

So after hours of fighting we finally won against them and they accepted defeat. "How about we go home to Earth and get a lovely big chocolate ice cream. I dibs first!"

Noel Anderson (10)
St Peter's Primary School, Newry

The Day Boble Came

In Egginbrough, Eggburt had his time to shine. He met his enemy Boble. He tried to run away but he couldn't, it was crowded. "What do you want?" said Eggburt.

"I want to rule the world," Boble said.

"Well I won't let you! I'm saving the world."

"Ha ha, good luck doing that!" Boble ran. Eggburt tried to catch him but he was too fast. But then Eggburt remembered that he had a supermoped that could fly, so he'd catch him now. Eggburt hopped in the supermoped and Eggburt pushed the button that could fly and *boom!* Eggburt caught him.

Ava Powell (9)

St Peter's Primary School, Newry

The Spilfs

One night on Mars, the footsteps of a spider were heard, but it was not a spider, it was a young clump running to its mother spilf.

The mum said, "Where have you been?"

The clump replied, "Uhh, with my friends," and sprinted off again.

As he was running, he accidentally ran on a galaxy path to Jupiter.

He was waiting for his mum.

The clump's mother already knew her clump was on Jupiter because she saw him running.

She followed him to Jupiter and they sat down, peacefully watching the wonderful planet they live on, in peace.

Gabrielle Lowe (10)
St Peter's Primary School, Newry

The Circle Lady

On Mars, there was a creature called Circle Lady. She was a crazy creature because she would rob places and jump and run away from jelly cops with her friend, Bacon.

One day, Bacon and Circle Lady went to Emm Park and they met Egg Man. He said, "Hey guys, what are you doing today?"

Circle Lady replied, "Huh?"

She gave him the side eye and then they started to hit each other really badly. They saw their friend Toast. He started to shout at the guy, and he said, "Stop you big Hig!"

Then everyone stared at Toast.

Evie Canavan (9)
St Peter's Primary School, Newry

Rippley Vs Sludge

Long ago in Lazy Lake, there was a superhero called Rippley. He was made out of water. He lived in a lake and had superpowers.

In stories, if there was a superhero, there had to be a villain! The villain called himself Sludge.

One day, Rippley was walking when... *pow!* Sludge arrived. People called for help and screamed! Rippley used his Ultra Splash, but it did minimum damage. Sludge hit Rippley hard, but then... Burn came to the rescue!

Burn made Sludge melt very easily and turn into a puddle. They lived happily ever after!

Conor Marron (9)

St Peter's Primary School, Newry

The Stretch Competition

It was two days before the Stretch Competition and Stretchy was very nervous because this year Stretchy's enemy was going to compete! Stretchy felt hopeless about the competition so she went to the super-stretch store. When she was looking around, Stretchy found a drink that said 'Stretch drink'. So she picked it up and drank half of it. She felt amazing. Two days later, it was the competition day, Stretchy was incredibly nervous as she stood up on the stage. She quickly drank and threw the can away. Stretch wrapped her arm and she... won!

Alice Johnston (10)
St Peter's Primary School, Newry

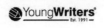

Jake And Ryan To The Rescue

Griffin Goblin was robbing Ulster Bank. Of course, Super Stewy came and stopped him, but for once Griffin actually stood his ground and fought back. It was a surprise but, of course, Stewy still won! Stewy was just walking in the town when he saw Griffin again, robbing a drive-through. Griffin tried again to stand his ground. This time, the fight went on for a long time and Griffin won!

It was mental, but then these boys called Jake and Ryan came and fought. Surprisingly, the boys won! "It was mental, but at least we won!"

Tommy McGlade (9)
St Peter's Primary School, Newry

Jelly Block

On Earth, there was a boy called Jelly Block. He lived with his beloved wife, Jemina, on a street called King Street. They lived together with their son, Michael.

One day, they were walking down the street and saw a terminal that took them to a crazy land called Crazy World. Their skin turned orange and they sounded like chipmunks.

They stayed there for four months. When they went back home, their skin turned back to its normal colour. They still felt weird in some ways, so they had to relax in their beds, and lived happily ever after.

Katie McGivern (10)
St Peter's Primary School, Newry

163

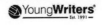

Untitled

In a faraway land called Mystery Land, there was Elene, a mystery no one knew about. She had claws like a wolf, spots like a leopard, a head like a horse, and a tail like a cat. Fred, the boss of Mystery Land, said, "Elene, I have a mission for you. Save Miss Princess. She acts like a princess, so watch out for her sass."

Elene said, "Yeah!" She went to the place, and Miss Princess was on Mars. She was hanging off the edge. She got off her horse, and she saved Miss Princess.

Fred said, "Good job, Elene!"

Sonia Olszowy (10)

St Peter's Primary School, Newry

The Bunny Who Could Not Hop

In Hopland there was an unlucky bunny who could not hop. Everyone called her Chubbybunny because Chubbybunnies can't jump because their fatness can't let them jump.

One day she heard there was a witch called Bunnitch the Bunny Witch. She was on a poster. She could do anything the poster said, even make Bunbun hop! This was a good day for Bunbun. She started going, it took ten minihops. She told Bunnitch her problem. Bunnitch sighed and gave her a yellow potion. Bunbun drank it. "Oh no, what's happening?"

Adaeze Obidike (9)
St Peter's Primary School, Newry

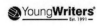YoungWriters
— Est. 1991 —

Milkshake Madness

One day, in the land of Good Burger, there was a cup named Cup Man, the hero of Good Burger Land. But, on the other side of Good Burger Land, Milkshake Man was hatching a plan to flood Good Burger Land in milkshake. The flood would start in two days.

"The countdown starts now!" said Milkshake Man. Two days later, the flooding began. Cup Man appeared and started a fight, but then a human picked Cup Man up and put him in the bin! Milkshake Man laughed and vanished from sight.

Chloe Carragher (10)
St Peter's Primary School, Newry

Chesty And The Letter Box

"Oh no, it's Letter Boxy!" exclaimed Chesty.
"Clamp!" shouted Letter Boxy.
"Why are you so rude?" said Chesty.
"None of your business!" said Letter Boxy.
"Can't we just be friends?" said Chesty.
"Fine but only if you give me a diamond."
Chesty had found a diamond on the floor
yesterday so he gave it to him.
"Wow, you aren't as bad as I thought."
And then they became best friends.

Kieran Fitzpatrick (10)
St Peter's Primary School, Newry

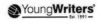

The Fight

Leah the Squirrel got lost in a tree with her enemy Grace. The enemy pushed Leah off the tree and Grace laughed at her and Leah was crying. Leah ran away and Grace ran after her. Leah escaped from Grace, she ran to her house and opened the door and hid under the bed and Grace couldn't find Leah and suddenly Grace ran too and they were friends now.

They went to the park for a walk and then they went for dinner in McDonald's. It was so good and then they went to lead Leah home.

Eve Connolly (10)

St Peter's Primary School, Newry

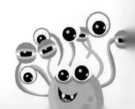

Mr T And Mr M

Mr T and Mr M were in Letterville. Mr T can teleport, and his enemy, Mr M, has robbed 1,000 shops and 10,000 banks. Mr T will have to jail Mr M for the banks and shops that were robbed. Shortly after he got jailed, he broke out and robbed a girl. Mr T found out and teleported to him. Mr M went invisible, and Mr T couldn't find him. Mr M then ran away, and Mr T went to look for him, but he got away and took Mr E, who was stuck in prison, so he saved him.

Michael Magill (10)
St Peter's Primary School, Newry

The Start Of The Great Apocalypse

In the night, a rift opens and the Devourer appears. It has eight eyes, sharp claws and a fearsome attitude.

"What will we do?" questions Bob.

"Fire the nukes!" shouts crazy Jack.

Nukes at 100 miles per hour hit the Beast but it just shakes them off. The Saviour suddenly appears from a rift and stares the Devourer in its eyes and runs faster than a super car and defeats the Devourer in one powerful punch. In the realm of flame, the Unbreakable is furious and sends Rags which are massive demon bats who kill the Saviour and start the great apocalypse.

Addison Balmer (10)

St Teresa's Primary School, St Helens

Skully Scare Saves The Day

Skully's fright sense tingles. So he teleports to the scene. His enemy (Illusion Master) tricks a civilian into thinking fear. Skully Scare doing his job, summons bones and Illusion Master retreats to safety. Skully bounces from side to side off his bones toward the ground. He teleports around the girl and then he scares the fear out of her mind. Confidence flies through her head and she is back to normal. Skully gives her a charm so she is never fooled again but reality collapses and Skully falls down and down and down. Skully summons the last resort. This shatters reality.

William Hobin (10)
St Teresa's Primary School, St Helens

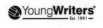

Mr Grey And The Colourful Giant

On Lonely Bridge, there was a monster called Mr Grey. Everything he touched would turn grey. Later that week, Mr Grey ran all the way around Lonely Bridge and turned all the houses grey. Mr Colourful Giant ran after him. If he had found him, he would've frozen him.

Mr Colourful touched Mr Grey and froze him. Then, Mr Colourful went around Lonely Bridge and turned everything colourful again. All the monsters were so happy because everything was bright and colourful again. Then, Mr Colourful flew back to his bright house. Everyone went back home happily.

Aya (9)
St Teresa's Primary School, St Helens

Her Virus

A little monster named Succy Muccy comes through the window, sneaks up to her and uses his suction cups to climb through her nose and defeat her virus. That's when he meets Drippy Bug, his worst enemy.

They both look at each other, feeling strong, and race to the virus, but Drippy Bug trips and gets tangled in some goo, and Succy Muccy gets to the virus.

He sets up and the virus glares at the light. Succy Muccy uses his suction cups to finish the job. He slides down the nose and out the window, back to where he came from.

Lucas Roscoe (10)
St Teresa's Primary School, St Helens

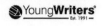

One Fateful Night

That one fateful night when she came back, she got her revenge. That one faint scream in that one empty house. In that one abandoned town. Why she did that is unknown but she said that she will only keep her throne. A wicked smile upon her smirking face. Everyone screamed at the sight. She glowed in the light, and always came out at night. Eyes opened with severe might. She really did always fight. That one fateful night when she was never seen again. Her sister suddenly disappeared and you realise it's a dream.

Rejoice Ose-Ose Ebhodaghe (10)

St Teresa's Primary School, St Helens

Eareac Beats Super Moon

In the solar system, there was an alien called Eareac and his enemy was Super Moon. He has an important job scaring kids and the last one is in Spain. So Eareac and Super Moon raced to go and scare the last kid ever. So they went. Super Moon was almost there so Eareac went to get a space taxi and it went over the speed limit and then Eareac was there. So then he opened his mouth and roared at him and was checked off the list of kids. Eareac was the best ever and his job was done.

Joseph Leigh (10)
St Teresa's Primary School, St Helens

Time To Shine

An overlooked, 'invisible' creature named Lucinda was yearning for a time to shine. Usually, her anxiety would insist that she stays unnoticed. One day, an opportunity arose in the form of a competition. *This is it!* she thought.

Two weeks later she was on stage. Lucinda was great! Suddenly, she shut down and sprinted off the stage. Embarrassment was lonely in her heart. Immediately, a teacher encouraged her with affirmation.

Lucinda regained her confidence and entered the spotlight.

A deafening applause congested the atmosphere as she bowed with contentment.

The next day, she started socialising! This was just the beginning...

Blessing Folarin (10)

Stifford Clays Primary School, Stifford Clays

Joy And Julia

Julia was sad. Just then, a bell rang in Happland.
"I'm on it!" Joy said confidently. First, she made her joyful potion, then she rushed to her rocket and flew to Julia's house.
Oh no! Joyless (Joy's nemesis) was just in front of her. Joy flicked the turbo switch on her rocket, so she got there first. She swiftly poured her runny, blue potion into Julia's bowl of cereal.
Joy watched happily as a huge smile spread across Julia's face! Just as Joy was about to leave, Julia caught sight of her.
"Thank you," she whispered.
Joy smiled and left. Mission accomplished!

Abigail Anyia (10)
Stifford Clays Primary School, Stifford Clays

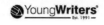

Monster War

One day there lived a monster called Fuzzy. He worked for the leader of Planet Pluto at the age of four. Mike Fuzzy's boss asked Fuzzy to do a mission to defeat the leader of Mercury and their fighters so only good monsters live in the solar system. Invisible Yetti and Shape Shifting Dragon are Mercury's strongest fighters, unlike Laser Beam Bat. They are the only Mercury fighters but Fuzzy is not afraid.

"Here comes the doom," said the monsters.

It was three against one. Fuzzy hypnotised Dragon then turned to the giant to step on the bat and Invisible Yetti. Now there were only good monsters.

Gracie Cook (9)

Stifford Clays Primary School, Stifford Clays

A Monster Against The World

Once upon a time, there lived a five-eyed, naughty monster called Rose. She lived in a large city called Monstish. Her favourite trick was to levitate others five inches above the dirty, hard ground. Rose's enemy is called Amber.

Amber said, "Hey, you idiot, go away!"

She hates Rose, and Rose hates Amber. But don't worry; Rose's friend is called Chocolate. Chocolate is very thoughtful, kind, and respectful, so that means that she stands up for Rose when Amber is horrible to Rose. The end, or is it? Don't worry, the end is not quite yet, or maybe it is!

Amber Waterman (10)

Stifford Clays Primary School, Stifford Clays

The Boggart Comes For Breakfast

I was awoken by the astonishing aroma of bacon and pancakes being cooked in the kitchen. I tiptoed down the stairs. I could hear the eerie clanging and banging of pots and pans coming from the echoey kitchen.

I knew it couldn't have been Mum, as she was away on business... I cautiously opened the kitchen door just a little and, on the table, I saw a banquet of golden pancakes, scrumptious bacon and syrup. I opened the door wider and, in front of me, stood a ginger, fluffy, five-eyed, four-legged, three-foot boggart.

Our eyes met. She screamed. I screamed.

Holly Seabrook (10)
Stifford Clays Primary School, Stifford Clays

Happiness

One day, there lived a monster called Fuzzy. She lived in Cuddle Land where there was joy and happiness. Suddenly, the moody monsters came out of the blue.

They said, "We are here to take over your land." Fuzzy was not going to let them succeed. So she decided they needed more happiness in their life. She took them to save cats from trees, help old monsters cross the road and help at the monster market. They succeeded and all because of Fuzzy. They all became best friends and combined their lands. Fuzzy was delighted and everyone was happy again.

Rosie Austen (10)
Stifford Clays Primary School, Stifford Clays

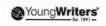

The Day The Earth Shook

One day a short five-eyed monster flew down from Mars. Jasmine was her name, she'd thought that she would get picked on by being transported by an ooglie googley. After a while, Jasmine was busting to show her trick and that was to do a handstand for two days. Before long, Bob The Burger King (her enemy) knocked her off the ground. "Hey, why did you do that?" she said whilst trying to say it cutely. Bob crouched down to Jasmine's height, Jasmine grew more confident in showing people great jobs.

Poppy Atkin (10)
Stifford Clays Primary School, Stifford Clays

Angry Crazy Creature

This scary, red creature is very angry because it appeared under my bed and I caught it. It was trying to eat all of my favourite snacks. His cheeks were bloated out like two balloons that had just been filled with air. I screamed and the big red monster spit green froth from its mouth. He scuttled from under my bed so fast I could only see his tail. I searched my whole house for this red, scary creature but he was nowhere to be found, I thought I was dreaming until the next day when my mum screamed.

Annie Smith (10)
Stifford Clays Primary School, Stifford Clays

Missing!

One day on Carrot Planet, April Rabbit went to her house to collect the chocolate eggs to give to everyone on Carrot Planet for Easter. When she got there all the eggs were gone! April Rabbit looked everywhere and found Mr Fox asleep in her bed, covered in chocolate!

Tara-Leigh Morris (6)
Voyage Learning Campus, Worle

Kaboom!

On Jupiter the monster was getting lots of planets with his long arms. He was trying to get all the different planets to make them go *kaboom!* with all the people in them. He wanted all of the planets so he could do what he wanted with them.

JJ Murray (7)
Voyage Learning Campus, Worle

The Adventures Of Boop

This is Boop. He is a flying snail! He lives in the sky and he spends his time flying around, spreading love to everyone, so everyone is his friend. Sometimes he lands so he can play games with his friends. They all live happily ever after.

Lucifer McMillan (7)
Voyage Learning Campus, Worle

Cartwheel

Once upon a time, Mike Wazowski had a son called Jack. Jack cartwheeled around school and loved love. As he cartwheeled he spread love to everyone. So everyone loved him and was kind to each other too. It was a really happy school.

Lexi-Louise Chivers (7)
Voyage Learning Campus, Worle

Cuteness Travels To Planet Earth

Far away on Planet X lived a cat Squishmallow creature called Cuteness. The creature had purple eyes, a fluffy body and fluffy red and cyan hair. One day, Cuteness decided to travel to Planet Earth and be kind to humans.

Luke Baker (10)

Voyage Learning Campus, Worle

YOUNG WRITERS INFORMATION

We hope you have enjoyed reading this book – and that you will continue to in the coming years.

If you're a young writer who enjoys reading and creative writing, or the parent of an enthusiastic poet or story writer, do visit our website **www.youngwriters.co.uk**. Here you will find free competitions, workshops and games, as well as recommended reads, a poetry glossary and our blog.

If you would like to order further copies of this book, or any of our other titles, then please give us a call or visit **www.youngwriters.co.uk**.

Young Writers
Remus House
Coltsfoot Drive
Peterborough
PE2 9BF
(01733) 890066
info@youngwriters.co.uk

Scan me to watch the Crazy Creatures video!

f YoungWritersUK   **✖** YoungWritersCW
◎ youngwriterscw   **♪** youngwriterscw